MURDER IN THE
DAYTIME

BLYTHE BAKER

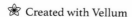 Created with Vellum

When Alice Beckingham returns to London to see her sister and niece safely installed in the family home, she hopes for some quiet time of contemplation. But she has scarcely walked through the doors of Ashton House when she is greeted once again by mayhem and danger.

A visit from a mysterious stranger offers Alice an intriguing concept, an opportunity to turn her snooping talents into a profitable business. And who better to join in her new venture than the clever and capable Sherborne Sharp?

But a sudden death turns Alice's plans upside down. Haunted by her failure to protect a client, Alice must discover who is behind a devious murder plot.

1

Sunlight streamed through my bedroom window, filling the space with golden light, unusual for late winter. It was a beautiful day to slip into my coat and go for a walk to the bakery a few blocks away. After a few weeks in Yorkshire at my sister's home, I was still readjusting to the many benefits of London life.

I pulled a flared hat low over my brown curls, slipped into a pale green knee-length dress with lace detailing around the drop waist and collar, and buckled on a pair of low-heeled two-tone oxfords. Dressing up to be admired was another thing I'd missed in the country. There hadn't been anyone to impress while there, so I'd opted for simpler outfits. Now, I felt like my sister Catherine during her society days, primping for a quick stroll around the neighborhood, lest the neighbors see me looking unkempt.

Content with my reflection in the mirror, I pulled open the door to the hallway and was promptly blinded.

I shrieked in surprise and fumbled with the thick, damp weight that was hanging over me.

"What is going on?"

"Oh, Alice." I heard Catherine moving towards me. "Stop flailing. It's just a baby blanket. And quiet down, Hazel is sleeping."

I huffed in frustration and, with Catherine's help, finally freed myself from the tangle of blanket. Catherine shook it out and rolled her eyes in annoyance as though she'd been the one trapped under a wet sheet.

"What was that doing on my door?" I asked just as I looked down the hallway and saw pastel-colored blankets hanging from every door frame. "Are you trying to booby trap the house?"

"They needed to dry and it is too cold for the nanny to hang them outside," she explained.

"We have a laundry room," I pointed out.

Catherine wrinkled her nose. "It's dusty down there, and I want Hazel's blankets to smell fresh."

"Like my face, apparently."

Catherine sighed and threw the damp blanket over her arm. "We planned to take it down before you got up."

"It's mid-morning!"

"Exactly." Her eyes narrowed in judgment. "You've been sleeping through breakfast every morning, barely waking up in time for lunch. If you'd kept to your new schedule, the blanket would be dry and folded in Hazel's room by now."

We both looked towards the door at the end of the hallway. The door to the room that had once been our older brother's. Moving his things out and placing them in the cellar had been difficult for everyone. Most of all for our mother and father. Aside from storing a few boxes in there, they hadn't touched Edward's room since he went to prison and then, later, was murdered. So, stripping the room of him entirely had taken several tear-filled days.

Now, however, Catherine's radiant bundle of giggles and coos had taken up residence, and she eased the pain in everyone's hearts.

Before Catherine and Hazel arrived from Yorkshire, I picked out a pale pink color for the walls, and Mama hired painters to make sure the job was done properly. Papa stood over the shoulder of the carpenter as he built shelves into the corner for Hazel's toys, ensuring everything was secured properly and safe.

And when they did arrive, Catherine organized the nursery with ruffled drapes and enough frilly dresses to go months without any washing.

We did our best to create new memories in the old space, to bring new life to it, not to forget Edward, but to honor him.

"You've been through a lot," Catherine said suddenly, pulling me from my thoughts.

I frowned, forced to recall my time in New York with Aunt Sarah, the time I'd spent unknowingly in the presence of my brother's killer. I shook my head, pushing the memories from my mind. "So have you."

Catherine's entire last year had been tumultuous, to say the least. She'd nearly died during childbirth, and then had spent months trying to recover, only to have someone in her own home attempt to end her life again. I could only imagine that kind of betrayal was difficult to move beyond, despite how cheery she'd been since her arrival in London.

She nodded. "We've all been through a lot...but that doesn't mean you should hide."

"I'm not hiding."

Catherine gave me a knowing look, one brow arched, and I crossed my arms over my chest, matching her expression. "I'm not. I'm really not. I've just been...tired."

"I can't imagine how after all the additional sleep you've been getting," she said. "Not to mention the fact you haven't done anything even remotely social in the week I've been here."

I opened my mouth to argue, but Catherine raised her hand and cut me off. "Taking a walk for a scone does not count, Alice. You haven't reached out to any of your friends since you returned."

That was intentional. It wasn't anything personal. I loved my friends, but I didn't want to be in their company until I knew what my plan was.

In the months since I'd last seen them, Dorothy had given birth to a curly, red-haired baby, and she and her Police Sergeant husband were in familial bliss. And Virginia had secured her first position as a buyer for a large department store, the first step on her path towards becoming a world-famous designer.

My friends were realizing their dreams, and I had only recently realized that I didn't know what my dreams were.

After visiting Catherine in the country, I knew I had no desire to live on a secluded farm far from the bustle of the city. Even the weeks I'd spent in New York had done little to satisfy the desire for *more* that burned in my chest. It was vast and exciting, but too far from my family. Too far from the people who mattered to me.

But did I really want to stay in London? And if I did, what would I do?

My mother would answer with certainty: marriage. It was what she had done and what Catherine had done. It was a sure way to find my path in the world. I'd latch myself to a man and support him on his path to success. But that sounded like torture to me. I wanted to support myself and find my own way, but unfortunately, that desire didn't come with an instruction booklet.

"You haven't reached out to *anyone* since you returned," Catherine said pointedly, chin low and touching her chest as she looked up at me from under lowered lids.

I sighed. "Not this again."

"I saw the two of you," Catherine said, lowering her voice. "He went all the way to Yorkshire to see you, and you are telling me that doesn't change anything?"

"It doesn't change anything," I said, stamping my foot slightly. My stomach growled with both hunger and apprehension. "I was just about to leave for a walk to get a scone, which is absolutely a social interaction. The baker seems to think so, anyway."

"Only because you're singlehandedly keeping him in business."

I gave Catherine a sickly-sweet, not at all genuine smile and pulled my bedroom door closed behind me, hoping to convey exactly how finished I was with this conversation. Unfortunately, as I padded down the hall-way, Catherine followed me.

"You've woken up today before nine which is a great

start, so I think you should continue this momentum and call on Sherborne Sharp."

Hearing his name sent a jolt through my system, but I did my best to hide it. "As my momentum is currently heading out the door for a walk, writing to Sherborne would only slow me down."

"*Call on*," Catherine corrected, taking the stairs two at a time behind me. It was remarkable that anyone had ever deemed her ill enough to need excessive amounts of rest. Since arriving in London, she'd been in non-stop motion, unpacking boxes, caring for Hazel, and pestering me. She had nothing but energy, it seemed. "You haven't spoken to him in too long and a note won't do."

On some level, I knew Catherine was right. I'd written Sherborne a letter before I promptly left the city without telling him where I would be. In response, he'd tracked me down and found me at my sister's house. Writing him another letter now would be a step backwards. And I only wanted to move forward. Whatever that meant.

Just not right this second.

"Don't you already have a child to raise?" I asked. "I already have a mother, thank you."

"Mama agrees with me," Catherine said.

I spun around, momentarily forgetting about my walk. "You and Mama have been talking about me?"

Catherine pursed her lips in a smug smile. "We've had plenty of time while you slept the day away."

As though summoned, Mama appeared at the top of the stairs. She was elegant as ever in a vertically-striped dress that fell below her knees with large black buttons going the length of it. Her hair was curled close to her head, pinned back with a metal clip on one side, and her lips were a deep red color that highlighted the pink tones of her skin. She smiled as she approached us.

"There are my girls," she said, holding her arms out. "I just checked in on Hazel, and the dear is still sleeping away. She is such a peaceful baby."

Catherine smiled softly in agreement, but I would not be distracted from their betrayal.

"I hear you are trying to marry me off to Sherborne Sharp, Mama?"

Mama gasped and pressed a hand to her chest, pausing on the final step. "What has gotten into you, Alice?"

Catherine hissed something at me under her breath that I could not hear, so I ignored her.

"That is what Catherine was just telling me," I continued. "She says you two have been having lengthy discussions about my future, and Sherborne Sharp is at the center of them all."

"I said no such thing," Catherine said quickly, turning to Mama.

"You did, too," I argued, furrowing my brow in a way I hadn't since I was a young girl. "You stood in that very spot and told me Mama wanted me to call on Sherborne Sharp and confess my feelings."

Catherine spun back to me, her face open and curious. "And what are those feelings?"

I narrowed my eyes, far too clever to be sucked into her trap. We were still staring at each other when Mama finally descended the final stair and came to stand between us, her smile from a moment ago gone.

"I cannot believe you two," she said. "One week in this house together and you act as though you are barely more than children. Bickering in the entrance hall, really?"

"One week in this house, and you two are already talking about me and trying to make decisions for me," I complained.

Mama sighed. "No one is making any decisions for anyone, Alice. And I don't know what Catherine has said, but we were not sitting around gossiping about you. I was simply voicing my hopes for you. As your mother, it is my right."

"I didn't say anything," Catherine said sharply.

"Lies," I hissed.

I knew I was being petulant, but I didn't really care. I'd been around the globe to solve crimes, putting myself in life or death situations, yet when I came home, I couldn't shake the feeling that I was the same young girl I'd always been.

And perhaps that was why I hadn't reached out to any of my friends or made any plans—doing so would be admitting that this was my life now; that I was comfortable with it. And I wasn't at all sure that I was.

"Enough," Mama said, slashing her arms down to her sides. "I do not know what started this spat, but it ends now, do you hear me? I'm having a lovely morning, and I do not want to be cross for the rest of the day because the pair of you can't get along."

Catherine bowed her head, looking remorseful, and I tried to mimic the action, though I was still upset. My business with Sherborne Sharp was exactly that, *my business*. I didn't want anyone poking around in it because I still wasn't ready to poke around in it. Like the dough Mr. Freeman dealt with at the bakery, I felt it would be best to let the situation between Sherborne and myself sit and rest for a bit before I handled it.

"Besides," Mama added with a pointed look at Catherine, "I said no such thing about Mr. Sharp. Catherine seems to have misunderstood me."

I lifted my finger to jab a *ha* in her direction, but Mama silenced me with a stern press of her red lips before continuing. "I'm sure he is a...suitable young man," she said, failing to hide how little she believed in her own words. "But from what I saw of him during our time in Scotland, he is a man who thrives on attention, especially female attention. I do not think he is the kind of man a nice girl like you would be happy with, Alice."

Mama would have much worse things to say about Sherborne if she knew I'd caught him rifling through her jewelry, looking for something to steal. I'd long since forgiven him for that sin—he'd proven himself a loyal, trustworthy friend—but Mama wouldn't forgive or forget so easily.

"He went all the way to Yorkshire," Catherine said, curling her fists under her chin, a moony expression in her eyes. "He dropped everything to find her. That suggests serious intentions."

"And where has he been since Alice returned?" Mama retorted. Neither my mother nor sister seemed to need or want my input on this matter at all, so with one eyebrow raised I crossed my arms and watched them argue about my romantic life.

"Alice hasn't reached out to him. She has been holed up in her room like a recluse. She has a stack of unopened mail in the sitting room. For all we know, he has been trying to reach her."

"Doubtful," Mama said with a roll of her eyes.

I cleared my throat and they both turned to me, blinking like they'd forgotten I was there.

"Thank you for your constructive guidance," I said, sarcasm thick in my voice. "But I believe it would be best if I made my own decisions regarding love from this point forward."

Catherine's eyes widened, sparkling. "Love? Does that mean you love—"

"I should make my own decisions regarding matters of the heart," I amended quickly. "If it should come to be that I do love Mr. Sharp, he will be the first to know. Then, if it is pertinent, you will know, as well."

Catherine smiled smugly, probably thinking she knew my heart better than I did—the way she thought she knew everything better than anyone did—and Mama frowned.

"Now, as your mother I think it is pertinent that I know these kinds of things first," Mama began to say, only to be interrupted by a firm knock at the door.

Before any of us could turn to answer it, Bessie, in her dark blue cotton dress and apron, hurried around the corner into the sitting room, appearing seemingly from nowhere. Though, by the blush on the maid's cheeks, I suspected she'd been listening in on our conversation. I couldn't even blame her. For years, I'd spent my time in the house in much the same way. And Mama, Catherine, and I were certainly putting on a show worth overhearing.

"I'm not expecting anyone," Mama said with a frown. She turned to Catherine and me. "Are either of you expecting company?"

"No one is here to see me," Catherine said coyly.

I frowned at my sister and shook my head, suddenly feeling the overwhelming urge to flee.

Bessie smoothed down her skirt and adjusted her hat before pulling open the heavy, wooden front door.

There, on the front porch, looking every bit like a handsome devil plucked from the shadows and dropped down to Earth, stood Sherborne Sharp.

Mama let out a small gasp, and I blinked at him, unable to believe the coincidence. Though, I quickly noticed Catherine was strangely silent and still. When I saw the smile pulling at the edges of her mouth, I realized it wasn't a coincidence at all.

"How may I help you?" Bessie asked.

Catherine rushed forward and waved the maid away. "Thank you, Bessie, but Mr. Sharp is a friend of the family. Please, come in."

Sherborne's dark eyes narrowed slightly before he bowed his head in greeting and stepped over the threshold into the entryway. He smiled at my mother, bowing again, and then finally turned to me.

His expression softened when our eyes met, and his mouth tipped up nervously in a way I'd never seen before. My mother wasn't entirely wrong to believe Sherborne was a man about town. He commanded attention wherever he went and moved confidently through life, which was why it was so strange to see him even slightly unsure of himself. Even when he'd shown up to see me in Yorkshire, I hadn't sensed any hesitation in him. Nothing like what I could see now.

"Alice," he said softly, tipping his head, his eyes never leaving mine.

I stared at Sherborne blankly, unsure what to say. I knew that Catherine was somehow responsible for his appearance here, but that did not mean I was any less shocked in the moment. I scrambled for something to say but words felt beyond my reach.

Catherine cleared her throat and looped her arm through my mother's. "I think I hear Hazel waking up."

"Really?" Mama asked, tilting her ear towards the stairs. "I don't hear anything."

Catherine's smile tightened around the edges and she tugged hard on our mother's arm. "Mother's intuition. Come on, Mama. Hazel always loves when you are there to wake her."

With that, my mother and sister excused themselves, and it became incredibly obvious that Sherborne and I were being set up.

The right words still eluded me, so when the silence had stretched too long for comfort, I sighed and said the first thing that came to mind.

"Catherine thinks we are in love."

Based on the surprised expression that moved across Sherborne's face and the immediate twisting of my insides, I knew those were not the right words. They weren't the right words at all.

2

M y face warmed, a flush creeping into my cheeks that I wasn't sure would ever leave. The heat only increased when Sherborne lowered his chin and took a step towards me. "Well, are we?"

Most definitely not the right thing to have said. What was I thinking? Clearly, I wasn't.

Panic set in, and I let out a loud, sudden laugh that made us both jump. My fists clenched at my side, and then I spun away from him and into the sitting room, talking over my shoulder as I went. "Would you like some tea? I think I'd like tea. I haven't eaten breakfast yet, so maybe some toast, too. Are you hungry?"

"I will be fine, but please, eat if you are hungry," Sherborne said, following behind me.

I nodded but made no move to call for a maid or go to the kitchen. I just stood in front of the fireplace, hands wringing in front of me.

Catherine was right on one point: I hadn't seen Sherborne since he'd left Yorkshire. He stayed for dinner the evening he arrived, slept in a guestroom downstairs, and then left right after breakfast. It was clear he'd come there to see me, and I made it no secret that I was happy about that. But then, he'd left, and we hadn't spoken since.

I glanced at the table next to the sofa and noticed a small stack of mail that was weighed down with a polished stone. Mama kept telling me to take the stack to my room, but I always found a reason to forget it or have my hands too full to grab it immediately. So, the stack had grown.

"I wrote to you," Sherborne said, breaking the silence between us.

"I've been busy." My voice was high-pitched and uneven, so I cleared my throat to steady it. "Catherine and Hazel have been settling in. I picked a paint color for the nursery."

He nodded and folded his hands behind his back. "You don't need to be nervous, Alice."

"I'm not."

He smiled, and we both knew I was lying. I'd never acted like this in front of Sherborne before. Our relationship had always been...defined. At the start, I blackmailed him into assisting me with my investigations. Then, he helped me willingly. Then, he became my friend. And now? I wasn't sure.

He sighed and paced around the back of the sofa towards the fireplace, taking slow, even steps. "Catherine wrote to me and said you wanted to see me, though it is painfully clear now that you weren't expecting me."

"Catherine thinks we are—"

"In love," Sherborne finished, cutting me off. "Yes, you said that before. But you see, I'm not very interested in what Catherine thinks. I'm much more interested in what you think."

What did I think?

I thought the sitting room was unseasonably warm.

I thought the walls might have been closing in on us.

I thought I would be covered in irreversible goosebumps if Sherborne took another step closer to me.

Just as he rounded the closest corner of the couch, no more than five paces away from me, I darted forward towards the mail I hadn't touched in over two weeks. "You wrote to me, you said? I haven't been checking my mail, as I told you. Let me look now."

"I'm right here," Sherborne said, a dark hint of amusement in his voice. "I can tell you what my letters said."

"It will only take a moment. Propriety dictates that I should have read and responded promptly, but as I said, I've been distracted."

Sherborne stood in front of the fireplace where I'd been only seconds before and crossed his arms over his chest. "You've never been exactly proper, Alice."

I flipped through the stack of mail, grateful for something to do with my hands. For something to look at aside from Sherborne's narrow, chiseled face and dark, piercing eyes.

"This is silly," Sherborne said, his voice low. "Alice, I went to see you in Yorkshire, and, at the time, it seemed as though you appreciated the gesture. Though, now I am not so certain. I feel I've made my feelings clear, but if you are still confused, I would like the opportunity to enlighten you further."

"Here's one," I said loudly, pulling a letter from the stack. I pointed to my name scrawled on the front, his penmanship sharp and angled much like his physical features. "How many did you send? I'd hate to miss one."

"Three, I believe. But as I've said, I'm happy to fill you in myself."

Sherborne's feelings were obvious to me. He liked me. I knew that much. My experience with men was not extensive, but I knew enough to know when I was admired, and for reasons I couldn't understand, Sherborne admired me. Even after I'd blackmailed him and been cross with him for no reason other than that his concern for me was a burden to my investigations. A wise man would have give up when I did not respond for over two weeks to the letter in which he first confessed his feelings. A less wise man would have stuck around a bit longer, but bolted when I finally responded to that letter and then promptly left the city for an extended vacation in the country.

But as the least wise man of all, Sherborne put up with all of my eccentricities and went to see me in Yorkshire and confess his feelings once again.

It was beyond time for me to be the one to express my feelings, but mine seemed to be jumbled in a single, immovable ball in the pit of my stomach. I couldn't disentangle them to save my life.

So, I sorted mail.

"Rose wrote to me from San Francisco," I said, holding up her letter. "You would like Rose. She is like you in a lot of ways. Very mysterious."

Sherborne took a step forward, his leather shoe squeaking on the hard wood. "I'm mysterious?"

I squeaked out a response in the affirmative and flipped through mail faster. "It will be a miracle if I have any friends left at all after this. So many have written me and never received a response. I should sit down and do this today."

"Perhaps after we talk," Sherborne pressed, taking another step. "I could sit with you while you responded to the letters."

"That would be dull for you," I said, tucking a letter from Dorothy at the bottom of the stack.

He chuckled to himself. "You have a way of making everything interesting. I'm sure I would enjoy myself."

My face flamed, and I blinked, trying to focus on the letters in my hand and not the ever-approaching shape of him in the corner of my vision.

When I managed to actually read the script on the envelope, I realized the name was not one I recognized.

"Mrs. Holworthy," I said aloud, thinking perhaps that would pull something from my memory. But no, there was nothing. _Urgent_ was written on the right side of the envelope, underlined for even more affect.

"Someone you know?" Sherborne asked.

I shook my head and slid my finger beneath the envelope, tearing it open. The letter inside was short and to the point.

MISS BECKINGHAM,

. . .

Your reputation precedes you. I have a case you will be interested in. Payment will be discussed when you visit.

Yours,

 Mrs. Sarah Holworthy

"Is everything all right?" Sherborne asked.

I skimmed the letter again, hoping there would be more information, but of course, there wasn't. Just the promise of a case and money.

And just like that, a path spread out before me.

It wasn't a long path, but it provided a next step. Something that would get me out of bed and away from the watchful eyes of my sister and mother. Something that could give me an outlet for the nervous energy buzzing beneath my skin.

A case. I could only presume she meant a mystery in need of solving.

"Yes, but I have to go," I said, tucking the envelope into the front pocket of my dress and moving towards the door.

Sherborne stuttered behind me, questions pouring out of him faster than I could answer.

"A case," I explained, answering all of them at once. "Someone has requested my services, and I must go to her immediately."

I grabbed my coat from the hook behind the door and shrugged it on as I stepped into the brisk London morning.

Yes, a case. For the first time in weeks, I felt grounded.

Capable. I'd never been summoned to a case before in this manner, but that only made the thrill of it more exciting. I was ready for this.

I'd made it down the steps and onto the sidewalk before an elbow brushed mine. I looked over and saw Sherborne keeping pace with me down the sidewalk, his eyes straight ahead. I stopped, and he took a few more steps before he turned around and looked at me, brows knit together in confusion.

"What are you doing?" I asked.

"We are going to work on a case, aren't we?"

"We?"

Sherborne smiled. "You once told me there was nothing between us but business. *This* is business."

"Yes." I stammered for an excuse. "But I later admitted we were friends."

His smiled widened. "Excellent. Then, we are friends and business associates. All the more reason for me to join you on this excursion."

I blinked, chewing on my lower lip. "But—"

"Unless you'd like to stay here and discuss, at length, the details of our relationship?"

The smile on his lips was devilish. My discomfort in the sitting room had been obvious and palpable, and now Sherborne was exploiting my cowardice to force me to bring him along.

And unfortunately, it worked like a charm.

I sighed and tipped my head to the side. "Come along, then. Don't slow me down."

Sherborne chuckled next to me. "I wouldn't dream of it."

IF SHERBORNE SHARP had not been standing in my sitting room when I read the letter, I never would have called on Mrs. Holworthy without advanced notice. I wouldn't have even written back to her without asking around to first find out who she was and how she became acquainted with my interest in solving crimes. Her letter had been brief and entirely empty of any clues as to what kind of case she had for me. Yet, there I stood on her front steps, Sherborne by my side, dropping the large knocker on her grand front door.

The woman was wealthy without a doubt. She lived in the same area as my parents, only a few blocks north, which made it even stranger that I didn't recognize her name. Mama knew most everyone around because of her connections with various boards and charities or through Papa. Perhaps Mrs. Holworthy did know my parents, and I'd just never been interested enough to learn her name.

Anxiety turned in my stomach at the possibility that Mrs. Holworthy would expect me to know her, and I would have to admit I didn't remember her at all.

I pushed the thought away and focused on what I knew.

Mrs. Holworthy lived in a stately, three-story brick terrace house. A small square of green lawn sat just in front of her home with a black wrought-iron fence around the perimeter. She had requested I visit her, per the note. I was going to be paid to take on a case.

I'd never been paid before, and the possibility thrilled me.

"You don't know what this is about?" Sherborne asked for the third time on our short walk.

I shook my head. "I showed you the note already."

"I know. I just don't like the idea of walking into this situation blind." Sherborne glanced around the porch, searching in every corner for...I wasn't sure what.

He gave off an air of confidence and swagger, but he was always the one attempting to rein me in during cases. He wanted to let the police handle anything dangerous and for me to stay out of trouble. Though he pretended otherwise, Sherborne Sharp was cautious by nature. And right now, he looked downright nervous.

"You don't need to be nervous, Sherborne," I said, using the same line he'd used on me earlier.

"I'm not," he said, standing taller and straightening the dark brown lapels of his jacket.

That assertion, though, lost some impact when the door was suddenly thrown open and Sherborne jumped in surprise. Admittedly, I jumped, as well.

The door swung open fully and a housemaid stood before us. Just as we were requesting to see Mrs. Holworthy, our words were interrupted by the arrival of another woman, undoubtedly the mistress of the house herself, who waved away the maid and took over.

A frail woman dripping in fabric and patterns and jewelry, her face was wrinkled, hands spotted with age, but she had bright green eyes and wore an intimidating smile.

"Miss Beckingham, I wondered if you'd come."

I glanced at Sherborne, who looked just as confused as I felt, and then back to the woman. I did my best to find my manners.

"Mrs. Holworthy?" I asked, forehead wrinkling.

"The very one," she said. "I wrote you many days ago. I expected you'd come sooner."

I started to say something about not checking my mail, but the woman waved away my words and ushered us inside. "Come in. We have much to discuss."

Her home smelled of cinnamon and something deeper...more earthy. It almost smelled like a campfire.

Mrs. Holworthy closed the door behind us. As the housemaid disappeared, leaving the three of us alone, I was grateful for Sherborne's presence. Moments before, I'd been wishing he'd left me to my work, but walking into a strange woman's house with nothing more than a sentence of explanation was not wise. Obviously, Sherborne had seen that and, as usual, had sought to protect me from my more impulsive instincts.

"I'm sorry for the smell," she said, taking small, quick steps past us, leading us down a wood-paneled hallway. "There was a fire."

"Oh no. What happened?"

"We don't want to get ahead of ourselves," she said over her shoulder, green eyes flashing. "As a detective, I'm sure you value the details."

"I'm not exactly a detective," I said. "I've solved a few different crimes, but—"

"I know what you've done." Mrs. Holworthy stopped suddenly, and I nearly ran into her back. Sherborne did run into mine, and he quickly stepped away, mumbling an apology.

Mrs. Holworthy opened a door and ushered us both into a small study. Bookshelves lined the walls, each shelf stuffed with leather-bound volumes, and a desk sat in the center. The desk itself was empty save for a single green-shaded lamp and a small metal container with a latch.

The old woman sat behind the desk, gesturing for Sherborne and I to each take a seat in one of the chairs opposite. As she sat, she reached for the metal box on the corner of the desk. With a practiced flick of her fingers she unlatched the box, pulled out a flat, circular white pill, and placed it in the center of her tongue.

Sherborne eyed the box, but Mrs. Holworthy made no effort to explain the contents or what the pills were for. Instead, she folded her hands on the desk and leaned forward, a smile tipping the corner of her dry lips up.

"I'm glad you came, Miss Beckingham. I expected you to come alone, and I will not offer additional reward for extraneous investigators. I hope that won't be a problem."

I stifled a laugh at Sherborne being referred to as "extraneous," a descriptor that made his top lip curl in distaste.

"I understand," I said. "This is Mr. Sherborne Sharp, a friend of mine. And a fine associate."

Mrs. Holworthy studied us both for a moment and then nodded. "Very well. You two will do fine."

"I'm sorry, Mrs. Holworthy, but we'll do fine for what exactly?" I asked. "Your letter was vague, so I'm not sure exactly what my purpose here is."

The old woman laughed and tapped the side of her head. "Of course. Your mind begins to loosen its grip when you reach my age. Enjoy your youth while you can. I intentionally kept my letter vague. I didn't know if it would be intercepted, and I did not want anyone to know I had suspicions."

She looked over my shoulder at the door, ensuring it

was shut, and then leaned forward, her voice low. "I believe I am to be murdered."

The words hung over our small gathering for several seconds as we absorbed their meaning.

"You believe you are going to be murdered?" I asked.

"Yes, that is what I said."

"I'm sorry," I said with an uncomfortable smile. "I'm more accustomed to coming in after the murder has taken place. I just want to understand what it is you are saying. You believe someone is trying to kill you?"

She nodded again. "That is right."

"Do you know who?" Sherborne asked.

Mrs. Holworthy turned to him, one eyebrow raised in obvious annoyance. "If I knew that, I would hardly need your assistance, would I?"

Sherborne released a harsh breath through his nose, and Mrs. Holworthy rolled her eyes, turning her full attention back to me. "I am a wealthy woman whose husband died years ago. My inheritance is vast, and I suspect someone wants to hurry along the apportioning of my assets."

"One of your children?" I asked.

She shook her head. "My son was killed in the war, and my daughter died a few years ago. Sickness."

"My sympathies," I said.

She pursed her lips in silent thanks and continued. "I mentioned a fire when you arrived, and I believe that was the first attempt made on my life. The fire was set just outside of my private sitting room when I was supposed to be the only one home, aside from my three grandchildren who were resting upstairs."

"Do your grandchildren live with you?" Sherborne asked.

"Yes, but they did not start the fire," Mrs. Holworthy snapped. "They are only children."

"I would never suggest it." Sherborne held up his hands as if in surrender and leaned further down in his chair. Apparently, Mrs. Holworthy did not appreciate his presence, and his keen detective skills, which she clearly doubted, had picked up on that animosity.

"My son-in-law lives with me, as well. He moved in after my daughter died—he and the girls—but he was out the afternoon of the fire."

We had only just begun discussing the case, but already I felt out of my depth. I did not know Mrs. Holworthy but based upon the fineness of her home, she was worth a great deal of money. Surely, she had enough to hire a proper detective. I didn't understand why she would call on me.

"I'm sorry, Mrs. Holworthy, but I'm still not entirely sure why I'm here."

She sighed. "I've explained it twice now, but I will say it a third time if I must: I believe I am going to be murdered."

"No," I said, waving my hand. "I understand that perfectly, but I do not understand why you are asking me to assist you when it appears you have the means to hire the finest detective in London."

"I could hire every single detective in London," she said. "I have the money to keep them all on retainer indefinitely, and I would do that if I did not believe it would be discovered. You see, I suspect someone close to me wants me dead. If that person discovered I was hiring detectives, they could seek to hasten their plans. So, in order to keep my inquiry covert, I wanted to employ someone capable who would also go unnoticed. Someone without the prestige of the best detective in London. I wanted to hire someone entirely unknown. That is why I wrote to you."

"How did you hear of me?" I asked. "As you said, I am not a prestigious detective."

"Mr. Williamson."

"The owner of The Royal Coliseum?" Sherborne asked, brow furrowed.

Mrs. Holworthy wrinkled her nose in his direction and nodded. "Yes. He is a friend of mine, and he mentioned to me that a young woman saved his theatre from closing when she solved the case of who murdered that famous young actor. Recently, I reached out to inquire about who the young lady was, and Mr. Williamson was all too happy to give me your address."

I would need to speak with Mr. Williamson about handing out my contact information to strangers without consulting me, but in this case, Mrs. Holworthy seemed harmless. At worst, she was a delusional old woman with paranoia. At best, a paying client.

"I did solve that case, but no one's life was actively in danger," I admitted. "The victim had already been lost, and I simply sifted through the evidence."

"You did more than that," Sherborne said. He leaned towards Mrs. Holworthy, palms pressed together. "Alice did a fine job on that case."

"You weren't there to assist me on that one, Sherborne."

"Yes, but I am familiar with the particulars," he said tensely.

"Thank you. Thank you both, in fact, for believing in me, but Mrs. Holworthy, if you truly believe your life is in danger, I think you should reach out to a professional."

The old woman lifted her chin in defiance and shook her head. "I've told you how I feel about that matter. My mind is made up. It is you or no one."

I sighed, the air pressing out of my lungs as though a weight had been set on my chest. "I'm not sure you are being rational."

"I'm not sure you are," she said, cutting me off. "I am offering to pay you a good deal of money to work on this case, and you are turning it down. Why?"

"Because I think the best way to save your life is to refuse your offer and push you towards a professional." It felt as though I was talking to myself.

"You aren't giving yourself enough credit," Sherborne said.

I snapped my attention to him, my teeth ground together, my jaw set. "As the extraneous investigator here, this does not concern you."

His eyes narrowed, but Mrs. Holworthy spoke before he could make any response. "Your friend has faith in you, and I do, as well. If you will not accept the case outright, then at least come to a dinner party I am hosting."

I frowned. "A dinner party?"

"Yes," she said, steepling her fingers in front of her on the desk. "I believe someone close to me wants me dead, so I will be inviting everyone closest to me for dinner.

Come and observe, see if you notice anything strange. Then you can decide if you'd like to take the case."

I started to shake my head. I'd left my parents' house with the idea that this case could be a distraction for me, but being tasked with keeping a woman alive was more than a distraction. It was an enormous responsibility that I wasn't at all prepared for. However, before I could say all of this, Sherborne slid suddenly to the very edge of his seat, his long legs bent in front of him. He pressed his palms to his knees and nodded his head decisively.

"That sounds like a fair offer," he said, smiling at Mrs. Holworthy, who simply grimaced back.

"An offer that is not yours to accept," I pointed out.

"Come on, Alice. You seem to be the only one here who doubts your abilities. Besides, if nothing else, we are being invited to enjoy dinner in a lovely home with good company."

Mrs. Holworthy hummed in agreement. "I do throw a good soiree."

I bit the corner of my lip, wondering how exactly I'd gotten myself into this mess and if there was any way to get myself out.

Sherborne let out a weary sigh and stood to his feet, buttoning his jacket as he did so. "We accept, Mrs. Holworthy. When is your party?"

My mouth fell open, ready to argue, but it seemed the deal was being struck without my input.

"Tomorrow evening." The woman opened the right-hand drawer of her desk and pulled out a tan folder bound with string. She slapped it on the table in front of me. "I've compiled a list of everyone who will be at the party and their connection to me. You are more than free to do your own investigating, obviously, but this should give you a starting point."

When it became clear I wasn't going to grab the folder, Sherborne grabbed it on my behalf and then held out a hand to help me stand. I ignored his offer and stood on my own.

Mrs. Holworthy clapped her hands and smiled, leaning back in her chair comfortably. "I feel good about this, don't you? I think it is going to go very well."

Sherborne smiled at the old woman and then at me, and I shrugged one shoulder and nodded. "This will be... something, at least."

Sherborne patted me on the back. "That's the spirit."

3

When Sherborne arrived to escort me to the dinner, Catherine nearly fell over backwards. Her mouth flopped open like a fish, and she blinked at me wordlessly for a full minute as I slipped into my coat and grabbed a clutch.

"I could have lent you a dress," she finally stammered. "Or done your hair. Oh, Alice, your hair. It looks just like you usually do it."

"That was the intention," I said quietly, looking to the door where Sherborne stood talking with my mother and father.

He looked every bit a gentleman, his long arms tucked behind his back, his head held high, shoulders back. He'd smoothed his dark hair to one side and wore a dark blue suit and a friendly smile. This dinner party already felt too much like a romantic engagement for my liking, so I'd kept my appearance understated intentionally.

My hair was curled and held close to my head with a

simple silver headband, and my cheeks were dusted a light pink with a similarly nude shade on my lips. Wearing an elegant dress couldn't be helped. We were heading to a formal dinner party, and I didn't want to stand out, so it was a knee-length silver number with shining details around the high-neckline and hem. My coat and shoes were both black.

"You kept this from me because you didn't want to admit I was right," Catherine whispered, positioning Hazel high on her shoulder and patting her back. "The two of you are a couple, aren't you? I knew asking Sherborne here yesterday was a good idea."

"You are wrong on every count," I said sharply. "You should not meddle in my affairs because I promise you, you don't understand them."

I wanted to tell Catherine why I was going to the dinner in the first place, but Mrs. Holworthy had made it clear that secrecy was important. No one could know she suspected the plot to take her life, and even though I didn't really think my family would talk around town about the matter, it felt better to stay quiet until I understood more about what I was dealing with.

Catherine started to argue, but I gave her a dramatic wave, sending the message that our conversation was over, and moved towards Sherborne.

"We should be going if we don't want to be late," I said with a forced smile.

Mama frowned. "Mr. Sharp just said he didn't yet know where you were going this evening. How can you be late for plans that have yet to be made?"

"That was my polite way of saying I'm done talking with my family for the evening." I tugged my frowning mother into a hug and grinned at Papa over her shoulder. "I will be back in a few hours."

They all stood in the doorway and waved as we left, and the expression of glee on Catherine's face paired with the contorted frown of concern on my mother's did not go unnoticed.

"Your mother doesn't like me," Sherborne said as we walked the few blocks to Mrs. Holworthy's home. "Are you sure you didn't tell her you caught me trying to steal her jewelry that once?"

I shrugged. "I'm sure, but it might be time to face that you simply have that effect on women. Mrs. Holworthy didn't seem to like you, either."

"She called me extraneous," he said, lower lip pouted out.

I laughed at the memory. "Yet you still agreed to take on her case. Why is that?"

"Because she is a paying client."

"A client paying me," I reminded him. "She won't be paying you, so why do you care?"

"It's good experience for you," he said. "Good exposure."

"Exposure for what?"

Sherborne turned to me, dark brows lowered like he thought I was being purposefully obtuse. "For your career as a detective. That is your aspiration, is it not?"

It was my turn to stare at him as though he was obtuse. "My career? I don't remember making that decision."

"You've done nothing but solve various murders this entire year. You went to New York and Yorkshire to unravel mysteries. It seems obvious to me that is your next move, is it not?"

I shook my head before I could even let the question sink in. "Rose and Achilles are detectives, but I am not like them. I've just been helping out family and friends."

My cousin Rose led an exciting life from the very start. She had an unconventional upbringing and was thrust into a tragic mystery she had no choice but to unravel. Then, she met the famous London detective Achilles Prideaux, and they teamed up—a dynamic crime-fighting duo. I admired Rose's tenacity and adventurous spirit, and I had tried to emulate it in some ways, but I wouldn't go so far as to think I could be a detective, as well. Which was why I resisted taking on Mrs. Holworthy's case from the start. She needed a true detective, and I was certainly not one.

"You aren't like them," Sherborne agreed, surprising me. Then, suddenly, his hand was wrapped around my wrist, and he circled my arm around his, his warm palm lying over my wrist. "You are like you, and that is even better as far as I'm concerned."

His words were warm and genuine, but they didn't make me feel better. If anything, I felt more like a fraud than ever. I'd fooled everyone, and going to this dinner was a horrible mistake. I tried to pull my arm away, but Sherborne tightened his grip and spoke through the corner of his mouth. "Mrs. Holworthy's house is just ahead, and we want to look like a couple lest any of the guests spot us outside."

He was right, and I sighed. This was another reason I couldn't be a professional detective. My emotions had just clouded my judgment. How was I meant to keep Mrs.

Holworthy safe when half of my mind was constantly on Sherborne Sharp?

I glanced up at him out of the corner of my eye, and he was smiling down at me. "Are you ready, Alice?"

Not even a little bit. Still, I took a deep breath and nodded. "I'm ready."

∼

WE MET Mrs. Holworthy at The Royal Coliseum.

Or, at least, that was what she told the guests she'd assembled at her home.

"Miss Beckingham and Mr. Sharp are friends of Mr. Williamson, the owner of the theatre, and he introduced us when I went to that play months ago. You know, the one where the lead actor was killed?"

Mrs. Holworthy told a convincing lie. She wove in just enough of the truth that it sounded perfectly believable, and her guests showed no signs of doubting her story.

"Crushed by an overhead light—what a gruesome way to go." The elderly man, introduced to us as Robert Wade, pulled on the bow tie around his neck as though it was suddenly too tight. "I had tickets for that showing, but came down with a cough and didn't go. I've never been so thankful for an illness in all my life."

The folder listed Robert Wade as Mrs. Holworthy's oldest and closest friend. When her husband died over twenty years earlier, Robert Wade stepped up as a close confidante and business partner. Mrs. Holworthy had funded many of his real estate ventures in the years since.

"Alice was there that evening," Sherborne said, nudging me forward.

I took a sip of the champagne I'd been offered by a young, red-haired maid, and nodded somberly. "Yes, it was gruesome. Not something I'm eager to relive."

"Of course not," Mrs. Holworthy said. "Death is far from party conversation. We are here to celebrate the reopening of the Holworthy Estate, not speak of death."

"The two nearly went hand-in-hand." A young woman stepped into the sitting room from the dining room. She had long blonde hair that curled around her neck, and wore a gold sleeveless dress that complimented the warm tones in her skin.

"Ivy," Sherborne whispered under his breath just as Mrs. Holworthy confirmed the girl's identity as her great niece.

"What do you mean, Ivy?" the woman asked.

The girl sidled up to her great aunt and squeezed her elbow tenderly. "That fire could have overtaken you had the cook not returned from doing the shopping when she did. You were asleep in that room with no other means of escape. The consequences could have been—"

"But they were not," Mrs. Holworthy said, cutting Ivy off. She smiled broadly at her guests, flinging her arms out wide, great swaths of jewel-toned fabrics hanging like curtains from her. "I am well and the room has been cleaned and returned to its former glory. All is perfectly fine."

"Thank Heavens for that," Ivy said, beaming at her aunt.

Robert Wade stepped forward and laid a hand on Mrs. Holworthy's shoulder. "Still, I will never forget the chill that came over me when I heard Sarah's home was aflame. I thought the worst and rushed over immediately. It was the worst day of my life."

"Dramatics," Mrs. Holworthy said suddenly, waving Robert Wade away, sending him back a step. "It will take more than a small fire for me to succumb."

I couldn't help but assume the woman was speaking directly to whoever in the room she believed could be seeking to kill her. It sounded almost like a challenge.

Over the course of twenty minutes, the rest of the guests arrived. A local judge and his wife—Judge Carlisle and Abigail, and a friend of Mrs. Holworthy's late daughter and her husband, Joseph and Bertha Taylor. The only person still missing was Mrs. Holworthy's son-in-law, which was peculiar since he supposedly lived in the house.

"Is Andrew busy with the girls tonight?" Ivy asked, pointing towards the ceiling and the upper floors of the house.

Mrs. Holworthy's mouth tightened in obvious disappointment. "No, he is not home right now. Truthfully, I'm not sure where he is."

Judge Carlisle tipped his head to the pretty maid who topped off his glass and then leaned back on the sofa. "Has Andrew been keeping himself out of trouble?"

I thought the Judge's question was playful, but Mrs. Holworthy's shoulders stiffened. "As much as he ever has."

The Judge shook his head, and his wife sighed. "A widower and taking care of those three little girls on his own. It must be difficult for him."

"The nanny is with the girls now, as she is most evenings," Mrs. Holworthy said with a barely concealed roll of her eyes. She shook her head slightly as though dispelling a nasty thought and turned towards where Bertha and Joseph Taylor were standing near the fireplace. "Did everyone know that Bertha and Joseph were recently married?"

Everyone in the room applauded softly, and Bertha's round face flooded a deep pink color at the attention. She tucked a lock of dark hair behind her ear and scooted in closer to her husband, an equally stout man with a thick mustache.

"I offered to send her to school for whatever she could ever want to study, but Bertha believed love to be more important." Mrs. Holworthy's tone was light and festive, but her words felt oddly accusatory. Bertha must have noticed, as well, because her smile faltered.

"Bertha and my Anna became friends when Anna volunteered to organize the very debutante ball that marked Bertha's coming out," Mrs. Holworthy continued.

Bertha nodded. "She was the only reason I looked even halfway presentable and didn't trip over my own feet down the stairs."

Mrs. Holworthy smiled at the memory, her head tipped sideways in thought. "I raised Anna to be an independent woman, and I thought perhaps she could be a good influence on young girls, but then she herself found love and married Andrew at a young age."

The woman spoke as though her daughter had ruined herself the moment she became married, and I saw Mr. Joseph Taylor squeeze his wife's hand discreetly, offering silent support.

"What of you, Miss Beckingham?"

I was startled to be drawn into the conversation, and my eyes went wide. "Excuse me?"

Mrs. Holworthy leveled her bright green eyes on me, sparing a flicker of a glance at Sherborne. "You are a young woman with a bright future ahead of you. Do you intend to seek an education or will you squander it all on something as fickle as romance?"

"Sarah," Judge Carlisle said with a chuckle. "We haven't even reached the dinner portion of the evening, and you are already subjecting these poor young ladies to your speeches."

"I have wisdom that I'd like to share before I'm dead and buried," Mrs. Holworthy said. Only Sherborne and myself knew how very soon that day could be. "I believe it is good for a woman to learn to take care of herself before she spends her time taking care of others. If they don't, they will never learn any different. Heaven knows a man will never press the matter. They are happy to be doted on and cared for by a simple woman whose only aim is their pleasure."

"You make marriage sound like a torturous experience," Judge Carlisle said. "Was Frederick really so awful to you?"

"No more awful than any man is unknowingly to his wife."

"Frederick was a good man, but Sarah makes a great deal of sense on the matter of marriage being restrictive for women," Robert said. "It is one of the reasons I am glad I, myself, never married."

The judge's wife, Abigail, leaned forward, a hand held to the side of her mouth. "They have this argument at every party. It only grows worse as the evening goes on."

"Take Ivy, for instance," Mrs. Holworthy said. "She is a girl with a plan and a vision. She will go to school next fall and earn her degree in Library Science, isn't that right, Ivy?"

Mrs. Holworthy's grandniece nodded and took a long drink of her champagne, her expression bored. Apparently, she was used to her aunt's long tirades on this subject.

"So, Alice," Mrs. Holworthy said, returning her attention to me. "What are your plans?"

Was I the one investigating or the one being investigated? It was becoming difficult to remember. Had there not already been enough people inquiring about this matter? Between my sister, my mother, Sherborne, and now a near perfect stranger, I was beginning to wonder if there wasn't a conspiracy going on behind the scenes to force me down a particular life path.

"I suppose I don't have any," I admitted with a shrug. "My plans don't extend beyond this very evening."

Mrs. Holworthy frowned and nodded towards where Sherborne stood. "And what of this young man next to you? You aren't thinking of marriage, are you?"

At that, I nearly choked on my champagne. "No. Certainly not. Well, I mean—"

"Our romance is new," Sherborne said easily, maintaining our backstory better than I could. Because we were meant to be a couple, and me spitting my drink across the room at the mention of marriage didn't exactly sell the story.

"A good man will wait for you," the woman said with a wink. "Remember that."

Oh, I certainly would. I'd recall it in tandem with one

of the more uncomfortable moments of my life. But before the conversation could continue much further, the front door opened and someone moved loudly into the entryway. There was a mumbled curse as the sound of someone tripping over something filled the room. All of the guests turned towards the door just as a rumpled man appeared in the frame.

He was young, but worn. His eyes were wrinkled at the corners, his mouth turned down in a frown, and his hairline was receding back towards the middle of his head. He wore a wrinkled suit and coat, and as if the stumbling wasn't enough proof, his eyes were bloodshot.

The man was obviously and entirely drunk.

"Andrew," Mrs. Holworthy said on a frustrated sigh.

He gripped the door frame and stood tall, his feet positioned at strange angles. "Sorry, Mother. I was held up by some business, but it looks as though I didn't miss drinks."

"No, it appears not," she said under her breath, only loud enough for me and Sherborne to hear.

Andrew Perring staggered towards the drink cart where a maid was chipping ice away from a block for his drink, but before he could get there, Mrs. Holworthy cleared her throat. "Florence, take the drink cart into the kitchen. Now that everyone has *finally* arrived, it is time for dinner."

The maid stopped what she was doing at once and rolled the cart out of the sitting room, through the dining room, and into the kitchen. Andrew stared longingly after it before turning narrowed eyes on his mother-in-law.

Mrs. Holworthy ignored him and smiled at her guests. "At last, it is time to eat."

The guests all filed out of the room in perfectly awkward silence, and Sherborne pressed a hand to the small of my back. When I looked over at him, he gave me a thin-lipped smile and whispered in my ear. "I can't imagine why anyone would wish harm on Mrs. Holworthy. She's such a pleasant woman."

I stifled a surprised laugh and followed the odd collection of friends into the dining room.

4
––––––

I did my best to monitor each interaction Mrs. Holworthy had at the table, but Sherborne's joke as we entered the dining room was seeming less and less like a joke by the second.

Despite the fact that Mrs. Holworthy was a very wealthy widow—money was the most obvious motive anyone would have for murdering her—she was also a demanding and domineering woman. It had become clear to me in less than an hour that she had likely made some enemies in her life, and any one of them could want her dead for any number of reasons.

Though, everyone at the table seemed to enjoy the woman's company. Save for her son-in-law, Andrew, who was so drunk that he didn't pay much attention to anyone. He simply slumped down in the seat to the right of Mrs. Holworthy and watched as the maid went around filling glasses with red wine. When she reached his glass, he swallowed down the first serving in one gulp and then gestured for her to give him another. The girl did so, glancing nervously towards Mrs. Holworthy all the while.

"Bring Mr. Perring a glass of water, as well," Mrs. Holworthy said coolly, lips pursed in displeasure. The young maid nodded and hurried into the kitchen.

"How are those little girls of yours, Andrew?" Judge Carlisle asked. "Last time I saw them, the eldest was barely up to my knee. I'm sure they've grown a great deal since then."

"Children are known to do that," Andrew said, his mouth pulled up in a half-smile.

The Judge laughed, but it was obvious he didn't find the joke very funny.

"I came by last week to visit, and Lucille, who is six now, played her violin for me. She is growing so quickly," Ivy said, trying to smooth over the awkwardness at the table.

"Ivy is a wonderful influence on the children," Mrs. Holworthy said, winking at her grand-niece. "Leona is just starting to talk in coherent sentences, but she is already talking about growing up to be just like her Aunt Ivy."

"A liar," Andrew said with a harsh snort.

Ivy's face reddened, and Mrs. Holworthy turned on him, one eyebrow raised. "Did you say something, Andrew?"

"That's a lie," he said, slightly changing his original statement. "Ivy isn't the girls' aunt, she is their...second cousin."

Mrs. Holworthy rolled her eyes. "Well, you can explain the complexities of the family tree to the girls if it bothers you so much. I, however, will call her Aunt Ivy."

The first course of the meal—a French onion soup—
was brought out shortly after, ending conversation for a
time as everyone ate. The Judge and his wife each
complimented the soup, spurring the rest of the table to
nod their heads in similar delight. And delightful, it was.
The broth was salty and flavorful; so good I could almost
forget why I was at the dinner in the first place.

The party was supposed to be a test—a way for me to
determine if Mrs. Holworthy had a case or not—but I
didn't see how that would be possible. Unless someone
pulled out a knife in the middle of dinner, how was I
meant to know who was murderous or not?

Andrew Perring was obviously the least sociable of
anyone at the table, but that didn't make him a murderer.
If I'd learned anything over the course of my time solving
mysteries, you could rarely tell much of anything from
appearances alone. The nicest of people could hold anger
and malice in their hearts.

Mrs. Holworthy was asking me to solve a crime that
had not been committed, and now more than ever, I felt it
was impossible. The longer I sat with these people, the
more overwhelming the responsibility became and the
more absurd the woman's request seemed.

When Mrs. Holworthy finished her soup, she laid her
spoon sideways at the top of her place setting, and the
maid came out at once to collect the dishes. Slowly, the
bowls were replaced with plates filled with tender game,
a deep red sauce, and a pile of greens. Wine glasses were
filled again from a new bottle of wine—a deep red color
—and once again, Andrew Perring drank his in one swal-
low. When he motioned for the maid to refresh his glass,
Mrs. Holworthy held out her hand.

"I think we should wait until the next course, don't you, Andrew?"

It didn't look at all like Andrew thought that as his eyes narrowed and his mouth turned down in a frown, but he stayed quiet, his fingers working around the rim of his empty glass as the maid continued around the table.

"So," Sherborne said, breaking the uncomfortable silence. "Mr. Wade, what line of work are you in?"

"Real estate," Robert Wade answered proudly, his chest puffing out. "I own several developments and have seen them through from the purchasing of the land to the final sale. That has been one of my biggest successes as of late."

"What of your biggest failure?" Andrew slurred from across the table.

Mr. Wade's face reddened, and Mrs. Holworthy's nostrils flared.

"Real estate is a fickle business," Sherborne said, once again absorbing the awkwardness. "Every person I know in real estate is constantly worried about the state of the market. I'm sure the same is true for you, Mr. Wade."

"True, indeed." Robert laughed. "There are so many hoops to jump through that sometimes it feels like a circus. There can be losses, but there can also be tremendous gains."

"Haven't quite seen the gains yet, though." Andrew cupped a hand around his mouth and hissed to the rest of the table, "Lost a whole bundle of dear Mother's money, he did. Come on, Robert, show us your ledgers. Where is that fancy briefcase you're always carrying around? Let us see what is inside."

"Andrew." Mrs. Holworthy shook her head and

reached for the center of the table. She grabbed a small metal case, and I remembered it being the same one that had been on the desk in her study the day before. She flipped open the lid, pulled out an oblong white pill, and tucked it into her cheek. Then, she quickly grabbed for her glass and washed it down with a long drink of wine.

She hadn't mentioned having any conditions that required medication, though that wasn't my business, I supposed. She wanted to hire me to find the person who may want her dead, not to know the details of her bodily health. Still, if I took the case and believed her life was at risk, I'd need to speak to her about keeping her pills lying about. It was an obvious weakness a killer could exploit.

Mrs. Holworthy wrinkled her nose as she set her glass down, pushing it to the center of the table. "I don't care for the flavor of this wine. Bitter, isn't it?"

"Tasted fine to me," Andrew said.

I suspected anything with alcohol tasted fine to Andrew Perring.

Robert Wade grabbed Mrs. Holworthy's glass and swirled it before giving it a sniff. "It smells just as I'd expect a Cabernet Sauvignon to smell. It is made from the strongest-flavored grapes."

Andrew clapped his hands slowly, pretending he was impressed, and Robert Wade pointedly turned away from him, ignoring him.

"Honestly, I've never cared for wine, in general," Ivy said. "I'm not sure I'd know the difference between a bitter and non-bitter wine. They all taste the same to me."

Bertha laughed for the first time since we'd come into the dining room. "I'm the same, Ivy. One glass leaves me with a pounding headache, so I don't drink it often."

"It's true. One glass and she is done for the evening," her husband, Joseph, said.

Andrew stood up and reached across the table for Ivy's still full wine glass. Mrs. Holworthy made a surprised sound deep in the back of her throat, but before she could vocalize anything more than that, Andrew tossed the glass back. "You must build a tolerance for it."

Ivy and Joseph stared at the man in twin expressions of horror, and Sherborne nudged my leg under the table. Whether I accepted Mrs. Holworthy's offer or not, this would not be an evening I'd forget anytime soon. I'd never seen someone so obviously and proudly dysfunctional as Andrew Perring. He seemed to relish the scorn his mother-in-law sent his way.

Mrs. Holworthy clicked her tongue. "Yes, it is an agonizing chore, but Andrew has completed the task with diligence."

Mr. Perring grinned at his mother-in-law, his teeth stained red in front from the wine, and Ivy laughed behind her napkin.

Andrew turned at the sound of Ivy's laughter, his red eyes narrowing. "If we are discussing one another's faults, perhaps Ivy would like a chance to speak. Anything you wish to share with the table?"

Ivy's eyes went wide, and she sunk down in her chair, shaking her head slowly.

"That's quite enough," Mrs. Holworthy said, speaking as though to two rowdy children who were picking at one another rather than two grown adults. "Andrew, there is no need to be so sensitive. If you don't wish for people to comment on your drunkenness, perhaps you should do a better job of hiding it?"

"Good idea, Mother," Andrew said, his eyes still on Ivy, sparkling like a predator who has its prey within reach. "I do wish I could hide things the way others can. Unfortunately, my feelings and vices are always on full display."

"Unfortunately," Mrs. Holworthy echoed.

The dinner party was beyond rescue at that point. No one wanted to start a conversation for fear Andrew Perring would take hold of the topic and make everyone uncomfortable again. So, rather than talk, we listened to one another chew.

"Would anyone care for another roll?" Andrew asked, grabbing the china plate in the center of the table and passing it to poor Ivy on his left. She tried to shake her head and refuse the platter, but Andrew insisted. So, the entire table passed the platter from hand to hand until Robert Wade attempted to give it to Mrs. Holworthy. She eyed the plate as though it were piled with dung instead of warm rolls, and Mr. Wade stood and returned the plate to where it belonged in front of Andrew Perring.

"What a lively bunch you all are," Andrew exclaimed later on as everyone was finishing their food and trying to find some other way to keep their mouths and hands busy.

I had taken to unfolding and refolding my napkin in my lap every few seconds, and Sherborne was shining his yet unused dessert spoon. Mrs. Holworthy seemed content to sigh and send angry glares in the direction of her son-in-law.

Eventually, Mrs. Holworthy called for the maid to

come and clear away the second course. "The cook made a berry tart that used to be my late husband's favorite."

Usually, I was more ready than anyone for dessert, but under the current circumstances, having one more course left before we could get up from the table felt like torture.

The judge leaned in to say something to his wife, his voice low, and Andrew cleared his throat and called down the table to him. "What was that, Judge Carlisle?"

The judge pressed his lips together. "Nothing, son."

"Then it should be nothing to share it with everyone," he said.

"Andrew," Mrs. Holworthy snapped, her hand hitting the top of the table. "That is quite enough. Stop harassing everyone."

Mrs. Holworthy had censured him several times that night, but for whatever reason, this scolding seemed to have an effect. As the maid went around the table, picking up places and glasses and putting them on her tray, Andrew stood, buttoned his rumpled suit jacket, and walked around the opposite side of the table towards his mother-in-law.

"What are you doing?" Mrs. Holworthy asked as Andrew reached around her and picked up her glass.

"My penance," he said simply, tucking the glass in the crook of his arm and grabbing her plate. "I have behaved poorly this evening, and now I will make my amends by cleaning up the table."

Mrs. Holworthy began to argue but quickly realized there was no point. Andrew gathered her place setting and Robert Wade's, taking both of their glasses, and turned into the kitchen. The second he was gone, the tension in the room seemed to ease slightly.

"I am beyond embarrassed," Mrs. Holworthy said, closing her eyes and shaking her head. "Andrew has been unwell for some time, but this evening has been...more than anything I've seen from him before."

"None of us blame you at all," Abigail Carlisle said, nudging the judge until he nodded in agreement.

"Yes, of course not," Judge Carlisle agreed. "We all know Andrew has struggled since Anna passed. You are a benevolent woman to allow him and his girls to live here with you. Heaven knows what would become of the children if it was left to him to care for them."

"Which is why I do it," Mrs. Holworthy said. "Those girls are the only thing I have left of my family now that my husband and children are gone. I care for them as my own, though I wish their father would sort himself out and care for them that way, instead. I hate to think what will become of them when I am dead and gone."

I'd never felt so much like an outsider before. Neither Sherborne nor I knew any of these people, and suddenly, we had been thrust into the private details of their grief and mourning.

"That sad day is a long time away," Ivy said, her lips pulled down at the corners into a frown.

"Everyone knows you are too stubborn to go into death against your wishes," Robert Wade said, making the entire table chuckle.

Mrs. Holworthy smiled and waved a hand at him, though it was clear she took the joke as a compliment. Then, her eyes narrowed. "Where is Nora with the dessert?"

Robert Wade shook his napkin from his lap and stood, buttoning his jacket. "I'll go and find out."

As Mr. Wade pushed through the kitchen door, Ivy slid away from the table, as well. "If you'll excuse me, I'd like to take this opportunity to freshen up."

The young woman walked silently to the swinging door out of the dining room and into the hallway towards the powder room.

"Good girl," Mrs. Holworthy said as soon as Ivy was gone, a proud smile on her face. "She is a gentle soul, but she has a vision for her future and a determined spirit."

"You say that as though a gentle soul is a bad thing," Judge Carlisle said. His wife sighed next to him, though she was smiling, clearly charmed by the bantering the Judge and Mrs. Holworthy often engaged in. "Believe me, I've seen many people come through my courts without gentle souls, and they would have been served well to be a bit kinder."

"I'm sure they would have been, but in many cases, the people those criminals exploited could have avoided exploitation had their souls not been so kind," Mrs. Holworthy said, raising one brow in a challenge. "Do you disagree?"

"I wouldn't dare," the Judge said, holding up his hands. "Not before the tart is served, at least. I'd hate for you to punish me by withholding my dessert."

"Well, then, I'll use your temporary silence to further my point," she said, chin raised. "When people are too kind, they are more easily distracted. They worry too much for those around them, concerning themselves with the wellbeing of others rather than the wellbeing of themselves. Like all things, it requires a balance. You cannot be entirely selfish or entirely selfless without seeing negative effects. I have sought to make it so Ivy will be a bit more selfish than her nature lends her to be. After the many losses I've suffered over the years, I know more than anyone that, at the end of the day, you have yourself and yourself alone to depend upon. If you want something, you must make it so without assistance. I hope to teach Ivy and my granddaughters that."

During Mrs. Holworthy's speech, I found myself growing rather inspired. There was a benefit in being kind, but not when one must forsake oneself and one's own dreams in the process.

"That is a rather bleak outlook," Sherborne said.

All eyes turned to him, and the Judge raised his brows in surprise. "Are you prepared to lose your tart, Mr. Sharp?"

Sherborne chuckled. "The main course was so delicious that I'm not sure I'll be able to eat anything more, anyway."

"Then feel free to continue," Mrs. Holworthy said, leaning back. She already didn't like Sherborne, so he was liable to lose his dessert even if he didn't disagree with her. As it was, I felt it was almost a certainty.

Sherborne nodded, a smile tugging one side of his mouth up. "Of course, there are benefits to be found in looking out for yourself, but no one can succeed on their own. Everyone needs help from those around them."

"Plenty of people have succeeded on their own," I said.

Mrs. Holworthy quirked her head to the side, eyes wide. "A disagreement between the lovers?"

My face flushed at being called Sherborne's lover, but

it was part of our cover. We were meant to be in a romantic relationship.

"It happens often enough," Sherborne said warmly. "I'm accustomed to it. I almost believe Alice enjoys disagreeing with me for the sake of it."

"Perhaps, but not in this case," I said. "I agree with Mrs. Holworthy. No one else has the interest in your success that you do, so it is best to go it alone."

For the first time, Sherborne's pleasant expression slipped. "You can't really think that, Alice."

"And why can't I?"

He blinked, lips pursing, and was about to respond just as Ivy came back into the room, smoothing her hands down the front of her dress.

"I hope you didn't wait on me," she said.

Mrs. Holworthy frowned and turned towards the kitchen. "We weren't. The cook is simply taking a long time with that tart. Where is Robert?"

Before she could even get the question out, there was a piercing scream from somewhere in the direction of the kitchen followed by the bellowed yells of a male voice.

Mrs. Holworthy's face wrinkled in displeasure, and she seemed to tuck her limbs in close as though she expected an attack. Everyone else turned towards the door, save for Sherborne who turned to me, a question in his eyes. I nodded, and we both stood.

"Who is screaming like that?" Judge Carlisle asked. "Is this usual, Sarah?"

"Of course it isn't," the judge's wife answered on behalf of Mrs. Holworthy. "Something has clearly gone wrong. Maybe a baking accident."

"We'll go see what the commotion is," Sherborne said, extending a hand to me.

"Yes, Alice. Go," Mrs. Holworthy said, urging me on with a flick of her wrist. "Do hurry."

Could this be another attempt on the woman's life? Before it had been a fire outside her study while she was alone, so attacking in the midst of a dinner party didn't exactly fit the pattern, but then again, one attempt did not a pattern make. Perhaps, the killer was desperate and willing to take out an entire group of people to get to Mrs. Holworthy. In which case, Sherborne and I needed to be careful.

Then again, maybe Abigail Carlisle was right and this was simply a tart gone wrong. An overreaction to a burnt finger.

Sherborne pushed open the kitchen door slowly and led the way into the space. The room was deep and designed in an L-shape with the main kitchen space in front of us and what appeared to be storage around the side.

I could see the berry tart sitting on the corner of the counter in a glass dish with a broken spatula next to it—split right where the wooden handle met the metal utensil. There was no one else in the kitchen, though the panicked voices that were muffled in the dining room were much clearer now.

"What is going on?" a female voice sobbed.

"We need to call for help," the male voice responded.

"Hello?" Sherborne called, grabbing my hand even more tightly. "Is everything all right?"

Suddenly, the red-haired maid rounded the corner,

her eyes wide and cheeks pale. Tears wetted her face, reflecting in the kitchen lights.

"What is—?" Sherborne started to ask.

"He's dead," the maid cried, dropping her face into her hands, her shoulders trembling.

I stiffened and dropped Sherborne's hand, moving around him. He held out an arm as if to stop me, but then lowered it and let me pass.

I walked around the corner into a narrow space with cabinets on either side. Some of the doors were open, revealing canisters of sugar and flower and bags of potatoes. All of that faded away, though, when I looked into the darkened end of the hallway.

Robert Wade lifted his face from where he was hunched on the ground. His skin was pale, almost glowing in the darkness. On the ground in front of him was a body.

Andrew Perring.

I gasped and took a step closer, wanting to help, but Robert shook his head sadly, his eyes heavy. "It's too late. He's dead."

5

"Dead?" I gasped, trying to understand how the man I'd seen mere minutes before could now be lying dead on the floor.

From the other room, I heard someone parrot after me. "Dead?"

Chairs scraped across the floor as the dinner guests moved into the kitchen, led by Mrs. Holworthy. Her head scanned from side to side, searching the room the way I imagined a bloodhound would sniff at the ground. When she saw me, she stopped. "What's happened?"

"Andrew is dead," Robert Wade said from behind me. I didn't see him stand up and walk across the kitchen, but now he was moving past me, arms extended to wrap Mrs. Holworthy in a comforting embrace. Just as he neared her, she pushed him away and charged forward.

"What do you mean?" she asked. "He isn't dead. We just saw him at—"

Without Mr. Wade kneeling down next to him, the sight of Andrew lying limp on the floor was even more startling. He looked so small and alone. Despite his abhorrent behavior all evening, I felt a desire to cradle his head and push him into a more dignified position.

I could only begin to imagine how Mrs. Holworthy felt.

The woman clapped a shaking hand over her mouth and shook her head, her gray hair trembling around her head.

"I came in to ask Nora what was taking so long with the tart, and when we walked around the corner, Andrew was lying on the floor just like that," Robert Wade said. "We didn't touch him beyond ensuring he wasn't breathing."

A strangled noise came from the back of Mrs. Holworthy's throat, and the old woman looked seconds away from collapsing.

"Come along, Mrs. Holworthy," Sherborne said, gently touching her elbow. "You don't need to see this."

I knew immediately that she was indeed shocked because she didn't protest at being led from the room. And by Sherborne Sharp, no less.

"We need to alert the authorities," Judge Carlisle said from the doorway. "Do we know what happened?"

The shelves above Andrew's head were perfectly in order. Plates were lined up vertically in narrow wooden cubbies and bowls were neatly stacked. Nothing seemed out of place except for a few empty wine glasses sitting on the edge of the counter.

"He finally drank himself to death," Ivy said, a hand pressed to her chest. She glanced up towards the ceiling. "Those poor girls. Both parents...gone."

None of the other guests had come into the room far

enough to see Andrew's body, so they were all looking between me and Robert Wade, searching for answers.

"There's no blood," Robert said with a shrug. "As I said, he just...collapsed."

"Did anyone check his pulse?" I asked.

Mr. Wade shook his head. "His chest wasn't moving. I didn't check beyond that. There didn't seem to be a need."

At that, I hurried forward and dropped down next to Andrew. On some level, Mr. Wade was right. There didn't seem to be much need to check his pulse. Andrew's eyes were open and glassy, his pupils had dilated, and his mouth hung open slightly, enough that I could see a bit of foam gathered on his tongue.

Gently, I pressed two fingers to his neck. It had only been a few minutes since we'd last seen him, but his body had already started to cool. My pink fingers looked garish next to the graying color of his skin.

I felt around for several seconds, and then turned and shook my head. "There's no pulse."

"He had so many vices," Ivy sobbed, addressing the group. "My aunt tried to care for him and his girls, but..."

Robert Wade crossed the room and wrapped an arm around her shaking shoulders, pulling her in tightly.

"I'm fine," Ivy insisted, wiping at her eyes. "I just can't believe this has happened. I've never seen someone die before. I'm shocked."

I wanted to point out that she still hadn't seen anyone die, but I decided to keep that to myself.

"Of course, you are shocked," Abigail Carlisle said, looking slightly unsteady herself. "We should go and sit down a moment."

"Yes, I'll telephone the authorities," the Judge said, seeming to remember that task all at once.

Slowly, the guests filed out of the kitchen, most of them without ever seeing Andrew's body. Robert Wade, however, stayed close. He leaned back against the kitchen counter and stared into the hallway. His blinking every few seconds was the only movement he made.

The kitchen door pushed open and Sherborne stepped inside again. "Mr. Wade, Mrs. Holworthy would like to see you."

Robert blinked several times before he seemed to register what Sherborne was saying. When he did, his mouth fell open and he nodded. "Of course. I don't even know what I'm still doing here. I should...well, I need to..." He sighed and walked out of the room without saying anything else, shoulders hunched.

"Interesting party," Sherborne said, all humor leeched from his voice. "It seems Mrs. Holworthy hired us to protect the wrong person."

"She hasn't hired us for anything yet," I reminded him. "I'm not sure she will now. How could we have missed this?"

"We didn't miss anything. This man put his problems on display for everyone to see, no investigative work needed. We were just unfortunate enough to be here when his vices caught up with him."

I turned to Sherborne, one eyebrow raised. "Is that really what you think happened here?"

Sherborne tipped his chin down, assessing me with dark eyes. "Do you believe this is more than an accident?"

I sighed and took a step forward, voice low. "It does seem oddly coincidental, does it not? That Andrew

Perring would die during the same time Mrs. Holworthy is concerned for her life? What if she misunderstood the threats against her, what if they were actually meant for Andrew Perring?"

He nodded his head slowly, processing the possibility. "It would depend upon the cause of death, I suppose, but—"

"Could be poison," I said. "There are no outward signs of injury, so it would have had to be something he ingested."

"Like deadly amounts of alcohol," Sherborne said gently.

I sighed. "Yes, it is possible he did this to himself. I'm not disputing that, but I also think there could be more at work here."

"It's possible," he agreed.

Before either of us could say more, voices in the dining room caught our attention. Seconds later, the kitchen door opened and policemen pushed into the room, claiming the scene as their own.

SHERBORNE and I were escorted out promptly by a young officer with a stern frown and a perfectly smooth chin. He didn't look to be much older than I was.

Bertha and Joseph Taylor had already left to go home, and Judge Carlisle and his wife stood in the entryway, talking with one of the officers. The officer smiled at something the Judge said, and then seemed to remember where he was and frowned in a thoughtful way.

Mrs. Holworthy sat on the sofa in the sitting room

with Ivy on her left side and Mr. Wade on her right. They were both comforting the woman, who was still and silent, her gaze fixed on a point on the floor.

As soon as Sherborne and I entered the room, however, her gaze snapped up. She shooed her two comforters away and waved us nearer. Ivy narrowed her eyes as I passed, clearly confused about why Mrs. Holworthy would want the company of a near-stranger during this hard time rather than that of her favorite great niece, but I just returned the look with a sad smile and sat next to Mrs. Holworthy.

"How are you?" I asked quietly.

She shook her head. "I'm not sure I can answer that question right now. I don't feel much of anything, if you can believe it."

"Shock," Sherborne said.

"I know what it is," the woman snapped, her dislike for Sherborne returning with a vengeance.

Sherborne met my eyes over her head, his mouth pulling into a frustrated frown, and I shook my head, trying to silently tell him I would handle the talking from here on out.

"Do you have any idea what may have happened?" I asked. "Did Andrew have any health concerns or—"

"Plenty," Mrs. Holworthy said with a bitter laugh. "He has been mourning the loss of my daughter for several years, drinking himself into a stupor before lunch most days. I'm not a doctor, but I know that can't be good for a man."

"No," I agreed. "I'd say not. Has he ever fallen ill from drinking before?"

"All over the house," Robert Wade said from across

the room. "The primary task of the maids for the last few weeks has been to clean up his vomit."

I wrinkled my nose in disgust at his phrasing, and Mrs. Holworthy, too, seemed disturbed. "Robert, please."

"I'm sorry," Robert said. "But I am trying to understand this myself. I walked into the kitchen in search of a tart and found a dead body."

"He was just lying there when you walked in?" I asked. "The maid was in the kitchen preparing the dessert. Wouldn't she have known he was there?"

"She did, but Nora knows well enough by now that talking to Andrew while he is intoxicated is a dangerous game," Robert said.

Mrs. Holworthy nodded in agreement. "I've told all of the staff to ignore Andrew to the best of their abilities. Like a child he acts out...acted out," she corrected herself with a quick shake of her head. "He wanted attention, and I was determined not to give it to him if I could help it. I mean, you saw him at dinner."

I nodded. "I did. He seemed...troubled."

"More troubled than usual," she said, her voice finally going shaky at the end. She lowered her face into a white handkerchief and sniffled. "I thought I could help him by ignoring him, but now there is nothing anyone can do for him. It is too late."

I laid a hand on her shoulder, drawing a soothing circle. "I'm sure you did your best."

All at once, Mrs. Holworthy snapped her head up and dabbed at her eyes. Her chin wobbled, but she stilled it as if by sheer force of will. "Robert, Ivy, would you both leave us for a moment?"

The Judge and his wife had left without saying

goodbye after speaking with the police, and the other officers were in the kitchen. Aside from the five of us, there was no one else in the room.

Mr. Wade turned and left obediently, but Ivy hesitated, brows knitting together before she finally walked into the entryway and pulled the doors to the sitting room closed behind her.

The minute the doors were closed, Mrs. Holworthy turned towards me, giving her back to Sherborne. "You must accept the case now, Miss Beckingham. You absolutely must."

Her green eyes were perfect circles in her wrinkled face, alert and determined.

"We don't need to discuss this now," I said. "This has been a tragic evening, and—"

"All the more reason to discuss it. My life is in danger."

Sherborne leaned forward, trying to see around the old woman's shoulder. "What leads you to believe that?"

She rolled her eyes without turning around. "A member of my family was just killed in my home in the midst of a party. Clearly, someone is trying to send me a message."

"But you spoke of his drinking habit," Sherborne started.

"To throw suspicion," she bit out, her voice quiet, but harsh. "If the killer is someone in this circle of friends, I wanted them to think I believe this to be a horrible accident. Really, I know the truth, and the two of you should, as well. The killer tried and failed to kill me, striking Andrew instead, and they will try again."

The quiet, shaking woman from moments ago

was gone. Mrs. Holworthy didn't tremble or tear up as she laid out what she believed to be the facts of the case. "There are policemen in there who will come to their own conclusion. Perhaps, that conclusion will reveal the plot against me; perhaps it won't. All I know is that I do not want to depend upon their findings. I'd like to conduct my own investigation."

"Wouldn't a worthy detective have caught the plot before your son-in-law could be murdered?" I asked.

Sherborne leaned even further around Mrs. Holworthy, his dark brows pinched together in a question I didn't want to hear or answer right now.

Mrs. Holworthy reached out and laid her hand over mine as though I was the one in need of comforting. "Only a worthy detective would have the good sense to doubt herself. You, Alice Beckingham, are the detective I want."

∼

"ARE you really going to take this case?" Sherborne asked as we walked down the damp sidewalks.

I didn't think it had rained—I hadn't heard any rain while inside Mrs. Holworthy's home, anyway—but the sidewalks were damp, reflecting the yellow glow of the streetlights. Then again, I'd been rather distracted. By the death of Andrew Perring amongst other things.

"Do you think I shouldn't?"

"It seems to me *you* think you shouldn't," he said simply. "You've expressed doubts from the start. Doubts you did not at all try to hide from the client."

I stopped walking and turned to him, looking up his tall frame to his face. "Don't you feel any guilt at all?"

He frowned. "Guilt over what?"

"We were asked to this party to observe and stop a murder, yet, a man was murdered."

"A man died," Sherborne corrected, one long finger raised in the air. "We don't know what happened to him just yet."

"And we don't know because we were too busy paying attention to one another to notice."

He took a single step back, eyes wide. "I'm not sure what you mean."

My face warmed. "Or maybe I was the one distracted. I suppose I should allow you to speak for yourself on matters such as—"

"I'm always distracted by you," Sherborne said in a low voice, his chin dipped low, looking up at me from beneath heavy lashes. He cleared his throat. "But that is not why Andrew Perring is dead. Whether this was natural or planned, the event was set into motion before we were asked onto the case. There is no way we could have stopped what happened after only knowing the people in that room for one evening. Even now, I would struggle to repeat everyone's names."

"Judge Carlisle and Abigail Carlisle, Ivy Holworthy, Robert Wade," I said, holding up another finger as I repeated each name. "The maid's name is Nora, though I don't know a surname. Then, the cook and—"

Sherborne chuckled to himself. "You do not need to prove how observant you are to me, Alice. I've seen you in action enough times to trust your abilities. However, I am observant, as well."

I folded my hands behind my back. "What have you observed?"

"Well," he said, pressing a finger to the underside of his chin. "I've observed that you only went and spoke with Mrs. Holworthy initially because you did not want to discuss the status of our relationship with me."

I opened my mouth to argue, but Sherborne shook his head to silence me.

"And I've observed you have doubted your abilities more times than I can count in the thirty-six hours since we first met with the old woman. This case is complicated, and only growing more complicated by the minute, and you don't think you can solve it."

I sighed. "I'm not sure if you are trying to convince me to take the case or not."

Sherborne stepped forward and gingerly touched my elbow. "I'm not trying to convince you of anything, Alice. I'm trying to make it clear that, whatever you decide, I'm not going anywhere. Even if you do try to ignore me and keep yourself busy with other tasks, I'll still be here waiting."

A chill worked through me and it had very little to do with the cool night air. I pulled away from Sherborne's touch and, easy as that, my decision was made.

"We'll take the case."

Sherborne blinked. "What?"

"You and I will work the case," I said. "We will help Mrs. Holworthy however we can, and when it is done, then we will talk."

He frowned and tilted his head to the side like he was suspicious. "What will we talk about?"

I gestured vaguely back and forth between us, suddenly too nervous to say it aloud.

"Our relationship?" he asked, lips pressed together in a suppressed smile.

I nodded. "Yes. We will work together on this case as partners, and when it is over, we can talk about being... something else."

"Really?"

The idea made my stomach drop. I didn't know what I wanted. Before the death of Andrew Perring, Mrs. Holworthy had spoken about following dreams and being independent, and that was what I'd been trying to be for the last year. I'd been trying to come out from under the mantle of childhood and become a woman in my own right. Was I really so ready, after barely more than a year, to tie myself to a man?

I nodded. "Yes, really."

Sherborne clapped his hands together and let his grin free, the smile splitting his face wide, softening the hard lines of his face. "Excellent. Then, let's get started."

6

"I'm sorry, I must not understand," Catherine said, blinking rapidly towards where Sherborne and I sat on the sofa in the sitting room. "A man died at the party you attended last night?"

I glanced at Sherborne, who lifted his chin in a quick nod, and then turned back to Catherine. "Actually, it sounds like you understand perfectly."

When Sherborne walked me home the night before, my parents were already in bed, and Catherine was tending to a crying Hazel. So, I'd slipped in without being noticed and gone straight to bed. Then, I'd avoided any specific conversation about the evening over breakfast, waiting for when Sherborne would arrive just after dinner to deliver the news.

My mother dropped down into the chair opposite us, her mouth hanging open, and my father lowered his newspaper just far enough that I could see his eyes over the top. Based on the slight raise of one of his eyebrows, I couldn't tell whether he was surprised or fed up with the nonstop cloud of death that seemed to hang around our family.

"We've been asked by the hostess to investigate the death," I said, leaving out some of the more sensitive information Mrs. Holworthy wanted to keep secret—such as the fact that she believed her own life was in danger.

Mama stammered for several seconds before she could form actual words. "But...you are not Rose."

I understood what she was saying, but the reality of her words still stung slightly. My cousin and I were different people in many ways. Namely that I was not a woman of the world married to a world-renowned detective. And I did not own my own detective agency in America. However, even without the extensive life experience Rose had or the assistance of a highly-trained detective, she and I had similarities. We each asked more questions than propriety allowed and were driven to want more than was expected of us.

I had a desire to solve crimes and nothing but my instincts to assist me, and I hoped that would be enough.

"I've only informed you of the case because a few police officers will be here soon," I continued, biting back the responses and arguments that were building in my mind. "The officers had enough to do cleaning up the scene of the crime last night that we scheduled an interview here...today."

My mother mumbled something that sounded like "crime," and then turned back to my father. "What do you have to say about this, James? Our youngest daughter is involved in a murder."

"Not involved in," Sherborne said quickly, easing the

harsh tone with a smile. "Investigating. Alice didn't murder anyone; she is trying to uncover who did."

"And what do you have to do with this case, Mr. Sharp?" Catherine asked. The day before, Catherine had spoken to Sherborne in warm, soft tones that sounded like she might like him as much as she wished I did. Now, her voice was cold.

"He is helping me much as he has in the past," I said. "Sherborne and I have a bit of history where mysteries are concerned."

Before anyone else could say anything, there were three loud knocks at the door, and Bessie came flying out from behind the door frame in the entryway. She'd appeared faster than would be possible if she hadn't been standing on the other side of the door, listening in on the conversation. Bessie answered the door and welcomed the detectives inside.

The men removed their hats as they stepped into the entryway and then folded them in twin poses against their lower stomachs. "We are here to speak with a Miss Beckingham and a Mr. Sharp."

"In here, officers," I said, standing and waving the men into the room.

Mama and Catherine rose to their feet.

"We hate to inconvenience you all when we have no reason to believe we'll be here long," the younger officer said, paying special attention to Catherine. Even with a ring on her finger and a baby on her hip, men were drawn to my sister.

"It's no imposition at all," Catherine said.

"Yes," Mama agreed, looking much cheerier than she

had only a moment before. "Whatever you need to do to resolve this matter. What a horrible tragedy."

"You might be the only person to think so," the other detective said. Gray hair dusted over his temples and deep lines bracketed his mouth. He curled his lips in an uncomfortable smile. "It seems based on what we've seen and heard that Mr. Perring was not well liked."

The younger detective stepped forward, forehead wrinkled. "And we're sorry if any of you feel differently."

"We didn't know the man," I said, easing his concerns.

Sherborne nodded in agreement. "Last night was the first time we'd met. And the last, it seems."

"So it seems." The older detective leaned across the small table in the middle of the room, hand extended to Sherborne. "Officer Burroughs, and this is Officer Howell."

"Nice to meet you both," I said as Sherborne shook their hands. "Please sit."

Mama and Catherine hurried out of the room, and Papa followed close behind, nodding to the officers as he went, leaving us alone.

Officer Burroughs sat back in an armchair like he hadn't sat down all day, and Officer Howell pulled out a small notebook, but he didn't bother to flip open the front cover as his partner began asking questions.

"Mrs. Holworthy said she met you at The Royal Coliseum?

"We were introduced through the theatre owner, Mr. Williamson," I said, skirting around the question. If the officers asked me anything directly, I'd answer it, but I didn't want to give up any unnecessary information about

the source of my investigation unless otherwise necessary. "He is an old friend of my parents."

"And she invited you to this dinner party when?"

I opened my mouth to answer, but Sherborne spoke
before I could. "We called on her the other day to visit,
and she mentioned the dinner engagement."

Burroughs nodded slightly as though this was confirmation of what he already knew. "Did you know anyone
else at the party?"

"Beyond Mrs. Holworthy? No."

"An eclectic group of people she gathered," Officer
Howell said slightly under his breath. "None of them
seemed well acquainted with one another."

I was under the impression they were all close friends
and acquaintances, but now that the officers had
mentioned it, everyone at the party had seemed familiar
with Mrs. Holworthy and Andrew, but not necessarily
with anyone else. There had been very little conversation
amongst the guests, only between the guests and the
hostess. Anyway, Andrew had dominated most of the
evening with his drunken antics.

"The Judge knew them the best," Officer Burroughs
said, speaking openly to his partner. All at once he
seemed to remember Sherborne and I were still in front
of him and cleared his throat, trying to regain some of his
professionalism. "Judge Carlisle is a well-known man in
the city, familiar with and recognized by many people. He
had more than a few run-ins with Andrew Perring over
the years."

"In the legal sense?" I asked, hazarding a guess.

Burroughs nodded.

"Mr. Perring was quite inebriated last evening," Sherborne said. "It became clear this was not unusual."

Howell tucked his notepad back into the front pocket of his shirt and leaned forward, voice low. "Mrs. Holworthy used her friendship with the judge to save Mr. Perring from criminal charges on multiple occasions. Judge Carlisle told us that himself. Of course, now the man blames himself."

"No," I breathed.

"Yes," Officer Howell insisted. "He was quite disturbed about the death last night. He thought if he'd hit Mr. Perring with the law then perhaps, he would have straightened himself out."

Sherborne frowned. "So, you believe it is drink that killed him?"

"That is the leading theory." Burroughs swiped a hand over his face and shrugged. "He was a heavy drinker even before his wife's death."

"Mrs. Holworthy's daughter, Anna?" I asked, though I already knew the answer.

Burroughs nodded. "According to one of Anna's best friends, Bertha, who was also at the party last night, Andrew started to lose control of his drinking when Anna became ill. When she died, he was a lost cause. He wouldn't listen to anyone, and he spent his time drinking and gambling his life away. Two years of steady drinking is enough to ruin anyone's health."

I frowned and Officer Howell misunderstood the meaning.

"I'm sorry you all had to be there for the end. I'm sure it wasn't the way you envisioned spending your evening. Or this morning, either."

"Not exactly," I said with a wry smile. Not least of all because I'd expected, if anyone was to die, it would have been Mrs. Holworthy.

Sherborne and I thanked the officers for their concern, and then they stood up, seeming eager to leave. It was clear based upon the line of questioning and the information they'd relayed that they were not taking the investigation seriously. In their eyes, Andrew died by his own hand—over the course of several years—and there seemed no reason for them to investigate further.

"Sorry to have disturbed you," Burroughs said, as though looking into the sudden death of a man was a waste of everyone's time. The two officers showed themselves out, and Sherborne and I remained seated on the couch.

"Do you think their theory is correct?" I asked.

Sherborne shrugged. "It's possible. Andrew died quickly—within minutes. It almost makes more sense that it would be something like heart failure than anything nefarious. I mean, he died in a kitchen while there was a witness present."

"The maid," I said with a nod. "It is strange that she was in the room when it happened. We should talk to her about what she saw."

Sherborne frowned. "Does that mean you don't believe the officer's theory?"

I could hear my mother and Catherine in the kitchen. Any moment, they'd realize the officers were gone and come back into the sitting room for a continuation of the earlier interrogation. Which, strangely, had been more intimidating and thorough than the one we'd just endured from Officers Burroughs and Howell.

"I didn't get a chance to really examine the body, but I did notice something unusual," I said, leaning in, voice low. Sherborne's dark brows pulled together in interest. "There was foam in his mouth."

"Foaming at the mouth can be a sign of a heart attack," Sherborne said.

"You're right, but did you have any reason to believe Andrew Perring's heart was failing? If he was truly drinking himself to death, surely there would have been some outward sign of his body's internal distress, but I didn't notice anything."

Sherborne's lips pulled to the side as he thought. "He stumbled and slurred his words, but that is typical for someone who has had as many drinks as he had."

"Actually, anyone who drank as much as he had should have already been unconscious."

"But he wasn't pale or breathing heavily. Perhaps, you are right and—"

Before Sherborne could finish, the kitchen door opened and my mother and sister came charging back into the room, expressions stern, ready for a fight.

"What did the officers say?" Mama asked.

"They suspect Mr. Perring drank himself to death."

Catherine hitched Hazel higher on her hip and pushed a small pacifier into her mouth. "So, you are done with the case, then?"

"Not until I'm content with the findings," I said.

Mama sagged under the weight of my words, her lower lip pouting out. "Alice, please. You've only been in town for a few weeks. Can't we just enjoy this time as a family? Every time I turn around, it seems some tragedy has occurred."

If my mother felt that way now, then I felt wholly justified in not telling her about what I'd learned in New York. Years after Edward's death in prison, my parents still struggled to pick up and carry on, so I didn't feel it was right to reopen their wounds by informing them that not only had he been killed in a prison fight, but the fight had been arranged by an international criminal. Who also happened to be the long lost American brother of their beloved niece.

"Catherine and Hazel are here, and we should be making the most of this time we have. Soon, all of my children will be out of the house with families of their own, and I don't want to feel as if I missed out on anything."

"I don't have to choose between this case and spending time with you. I have time for both."

Mama didn't look at all convinced, but Catherine stepped forward before she could say anything more.

"I'm more worried about the danger involved," Catherine said. "It seems to me you are meddling in matters that do not concern you, and you are opening yourself up to be put in harm's way. You and I both know very well that anyone who can kill one person is capable and willing to kill two."

Catherine and I did both know that. First hand, in fact. The person who had sought to kill Catherine in Yorkshire came after me with the same vengeance when I got close to solving that case.

And again, I felt justified in keeping many of my investigations separate and private from my family. If they only knew how many times I'd been in harm's way in the last year, they'd never let me leave the house again.

"That, too," my mother said, nodding in fervent agreement with Catherine's point. "It isn't safe, Alice, and I think you should turn down this case. If it is money you are after, your father and I are more than happy to do what we can to make you more comfortable. If you insisted, I'm sure we could procure you employment somewhere, though that doesn't seem entirely necessary."

"I agree with you both," Sherborne said suddenly. He sat forward on the sofa, his long legs bent in front of him. He seemed too big for every environment he found himself in, as though the world wasn't quite made for him.

I frowned. "You do?"

"Of course," Sherborne said, glancing at me before smiling up at my mother and sister. "As someone who is not in touch with his family, I understand the value of time spent in each other's company. I wish I had a mother and sibling who cared about me the way you two care for Alice."

My mother's cheeks pinked at that, but she didn't smile. I wasn't sure I'd ever seen her smile in Sherborne's direction. Catherine, however, beamed at him.

"And as someone who is quite fond of Alice, myself, I do not wish any harm to come to her for any reason."

At that, my cheeks pinked, though I hoped no one would notice.

If my family knew how many times my life had been in danger, they'd be horrified. But if they knew how many of those times Sherborne had appeared and helped to save me, my mother wouldn't be glaring at him in such a suspicious manner.

"However," Sherborne added cautiously, his eyes shifting from their faces to the floor. He folded his hands over his knees and sighed. "Alice is an independent, intelligent woman. She is qualified and capable of making her own decisions, and if she wishes to continue with this case, then that is what we will do. I will defer entirely to her judgment on the matter."

The room felt too still and tension weighed heavily on my shoulders. I'd stood up for myself more times than I could count to my family, declaring myself a capable adult, but I'd never had anyone stand up on my behalf. It felt nice.

I sat up straighter on the sofa and faced my mother and sister who were both now staring at Sherborne, brows lowered in suspicion.

I cleared my throat to draw their eyes back to me. "I appreciate all of your concerns, but I am going to take this case. Mrs. Holworthy asked me for my assistance because she believed I was the right person for the job, and I do not want to let her down. Know that I will take every precaution to ensure my own safety."

"As will I," Sherborne added. As soon as the words were out of his mouth, he was back under the watchful, angry eyes of my family.

I could sense a second round of arguing coming, so before anyone could say anything, I informed my family that Sherborne and I had a prior appointment, and after a second of confusion, Sherborne stood at once and joined me in hurrying towards the door.

Once we were on the sidewalk outside, he sighed. "Lady Ashton is a petite, yet fearsome woman. It must run in the family."

I smirked, biting back my smile. "I thought it would be a good idea to get back to Mrs. Holworthy's house as early today as possible to talk with her and the household staff. The longer we wait, the more jumbled their stories will be."

"Good idea," he agreed. "Once they all start talking about what they've heard and the investigation, we won't know what they actually observed or what is hearsay."

"Exactly."

We walked in silence for nearly a block before I looked up at him from the corner of my eye and said softly, "Thank you, by the way."

He frowned. "For what?"

I hitched a thumb over my shoulder. "For...back there. For saying what you said. It was—"

"The truth," he finished with a smile. "It was the truth. You don't need to thank me for that."

This time, I couldn't hide my smile.

7

Understandably, the Holworthy house was still reeling from Andrew Perring's untimely demise.

When Sherborne knocked on the door, it was a full three minutes before anyone opened it. Then, when we were shown into the sitting room we'd been in only the night before, it was another ten minutes before we were offered tea.

Nora, the red-haired maid, was nowhere to be seen. In her stead was a younger girl, no more than sixteen, with wide doe-like eyes and perpetually rosy cheeks. She seemed frazzled, her dark hair sticking out at odd angles, so we declined any tea, hoping not to make more work for her.

"Mrs. Holworthy will be with you shortly," she said, her voice shaky. "She has been upstairs with the girls all morning. Breaking the news."

When the maid left, Sherborne shook his head. "I

almost forgot about his daughters. This must be horrible for them."

Truly, so had I. Guilt twisted in my stomach. When I'd discovered Andrew dead, even though I hardly knew the man, there had been a tiny sense of relief that it had been him to fall rather than anyone else at the party. He'd been horrible all evening, and I wasn't particularly distressed at the loss of him. Shocked, of course, but not sad.

Now, however, thinking of his daughters who were without both a mother and a father, my heart ached.

Light streamed in the front sitting room windows, but the air felt thick with grief. And even though the overwhelming scent in the room came from a bowl of potpourri on the center table, I couldn't help but imagine the scent of decay in the air.

"Earlier, you mentioned seeing foam in Andrew's mouth," Sherborne said softly, pulling me from my dark thoughts.

The theory had been swirling in my mind for so long that I was grateful for the opportunity to get it out. "A possible sign of poison."

"Or heart failure," he said, repeating the police's theory.

"The police believe it was heart failure, and they could be right, but what if they aren't?"

"Very well, let's say Andrew was poisoned," Sherborne posited. "Does that mean it was his life in danger the entire time and not Mrs. Holworthy's, or do you think they were both targeted? And if so, why?"

Sherborne and I had shared information on cases before, but we'd never actively worked one together.

Usually, he ran off to fetch me a small piece of information while I did the groundwork myself. It felt surprisingly good to have someone to talk through possibilities and motives with.

"Either," I admitted. "If Andrew was poisoned, the poison could have very well been meant for Mrs. Holworthy. Perhaps, the killer miscalculated and killed Andrew by mistake. Or, Andrew was killed to send Mrs. Holworthy a message."

"How would he have been poisoned, though? We all ate the same food and drank from the same bottles of wine."

That was one of many questions I still had not puzzled out—not even enough to have a working theory —though I didn't want to tell Sherborne that. I could feel that he was leaning towards believing the official findings of the police, and I didn't want to say anything that would make him believe I didn't know what I was talking about.

Before he could press me to answer, we heard footsteps on the stairs, and moments later, Mrs. Holworthy came into the room in a flurry of fabrics. Her fine garments draped from her arms like velvet wings and swooshed around her body with every step.

"I'm sorry to keep you waiting. I've barely slept and now I'm beginning to explain things to the girls and—"

"No, I'm sorry," I said, standing up and reaching for her hands. I didn't know the woman well, but the situation called for some kind of physical comfort. Her skin was dry and frail against mine, but I squeezed her fingers. "We shouldn't have dropped in unannounced. Of course, you are busy with more important things."

"More important than my life?" Mrs. Holworthy asked, dropping my hands and sitting in the armchair across from the sofa. She crossed her legs at the ankle and arched a gray eyebrow. "Nothing is more important than that, Miss Beckingham. I assume the case is why you are here? You've agreed to take it on?"

She switched into business talk so fast that it took me a moment to catch up. "Yes, I have. *We* have."

"Excellent. That is marvelous news. As you can imagine, I'm rather shaken up by all of this. I'm not sure what to think."

"The police believe he drank himself to death," Sherborne said. "They think it could be heart failure."

She twisted her lips to one side in thought. "He certainly drank enough for that to be possible, but I don't want to make any assumptions that will cost me my life. I'd rather be cautious."

"I agree," I said. "Which is why we came here to talk with you and some of your staff. About the fire and last night."

Mrs. Holworthy frowned. "No one knows about my suspicions. It wouldn't be safe for them to know. For me or for them. Anyone who suspects the killer's plans could be at risk, which is why you and Mr. Sharp are the only people I've confided in."

"We will be discreet," Sherborne said. "The questions will be general, and we won't tell any of them that you've hired us."

She thought on it for a moment and then nodded. "That will be all right, then. As long as you are, indeed, discreet."

She reached into a pocket on the front of her layered dress and pulled out the same metal container I'd seen her with at dinner the night before. She placed a flat white pill on her tongue before dropping the tin back in her pocket.

"I've been meaning to speak with you about the tin you carry with you."

Mrs. Holworthy froze, her hand pressed to her hip where I imagined the tin rested inside her pocket. "What about it, dear?"

We hadn't spoken to Mrs. Holworthy about anything personal in her life, beyond her belief someone was trying to kill her, so I had no idea what could ail her that she needed to carry a pill container with her constantly. Based on the narrow-eyed look on her face, however, it seemed that the ailment could be quite personal.

"It is just that if someone is seeking to harm you, slipping something dangerous into that pill container would be an easy way to do it."

"That is clever," Sherborne said. "It would be wise to keep that close to you at all times."

Mrs. Holworthy seemed to relax slightly, and she winked at me. "That is why I hired you, Miss Beckingham. You are a quick girl. I'll be more careful in future. I won't let it out of my sight."

"Anything you can do to minimize your risk would be wise," I said, glancing around the room. "Ensuring windows and doors are locked at night, not being alone in the house, not going out alone in the evenings, and not hosting any events."

She scoffed. "It sounds like you want to make me a prisoner."

"My job is to keep you safe. That is much easier to do if I know who you are with and when at all times."

"That is fair," she admitted. "Besides, no one will want to come to one of my dinner parties for a good while, I'd imagine. Plausible explanation or not, death makes people skittish."

"I would imagine you'd rather be alone, as well," Sherborne said. "If someone is trying to end your life, you must feel safer on your own."

"Yes and no," she admitted with a shrug. "I was alone when the fire was set outside of my sitting room. Had the cook not come home, I could have died. Having those I trust close to me helps me feel more protected."

"Did you notice anything unusual that day?" I asked. "Did you hear anything strange or notice anyone behaving suspiciously?"

Mrs. Holworthy pursed her lips in thought, wrinkles puckering around her mouth. "Not that I can recall. Andrew left for the day, and he wanted to take the car, but I asked the driver to remain behind in case I wanted to take the girls anywhere in the afternoon. After Andrew left, the nanny put the girls down for their afternoon rest, I told the maid to leave me to a nap in the sitting room, and then I went to sleep. When I awoke, the cook was batting down flames in the corridor and screaming loud enough to wake the dead."

"Do you know where Andrew was that day?"

"No, I rarely do," she admitted. "He came and went at all hours, and at some point, I didn't want to know the truth. As a Christian woman, it was easier on my mind to remain in the dark."

I couldn't imagine Mrs. Holworthy ever choosing to

remain ignorant of anything going on in her household. She seemed to be the kind of woman who had her hand in everything.

"Things seemed tense between the two of you at the dinner party last night," I said, trying to broach the subject gently considering the man hadn't even been dead twenty-four hours yet. "I got the sense that your relationship was a tumultuous one."

Mrs. Holworthy frowned, gray eyebrows pulling together. "I wouldn't say that. Andrew and I argued from time to time as people who live together are prone to do, but I loved him as a son. He cared for my daughter diligently throughout her illness, even if he did indulge too much in drink from time to time. After her death, he stumbled. I was harsh on him because I knew he could do better, but that does not mean I did not love him."

"And I would never suggest you didn't. It is just that if anyone had motive to kill you, would it not be the widowed husband of your only living child? Who is set to inherit when you pass?"

Mrs. Holworthy swallowed, her throat bobbing. "Andrew would have received a large sum, but it would have been for him and the girls."

"The house, too?" Sherborne asked.

The old woman nodded as though it pained her to even consider the possibility that Andrew had been the one to try and kill her.

"Is anyone else mentioned in your will?" I asked.

"Andrew, the girls, Ivy, and Robert Wade are the main beneficiaries."

"Do you have any reason to suspect any of them?"

"Of course not," she snapped. "If I did, they wouldn't be in my will."

"I'm sorry, Mrs. Holworthy," I said, holding my hands up in the universal sign of surrender. "I know this is difficult to discuss, but you've hired me to look into who could want to murder you, and the sad truth is that most murders are committed by people the victim knows. It is most likely that someone close to you is responsible, so I have to consider every possibility."

"I know that." She sighed. "You are doing the task I've hired you for, and I'm sorry, but the idea that someone I love could want to harm me is just...it's unbearable. I've been like a grandmother to Ivy for years. Her own grandparents passed when she was young, and I stepped into the role of grandparent as I know my brother would have wanted. I've helped raise her to be the intelligent, independent woman she is today, and I can't believe that she would have any reason to want to harm me."

"And Robert Wade?" I pressed.

"No." She shook her head once, her jaw clenched and set. "Robert has been a constant friend and business partner for years. He would never—"

"Last night, Andrew mentioned Robert's business failing," Sherborne said, the sentence neither a statement nor a question.

"And Robert explained that the real estate industry is fickle," she said, eyes narrowed in Sherborne's direction. "I know about Robert's business dealings. He keeps nothing secret from me."

"Are you two—?" I couldn't even finish the question before Mrs. Holworthy lifted her chin in indignation and shook her head.

"He is a dear friend whom I trust. That is all."

According to Mrs. Holworthy, no one had any reason at all to want to kill her, so we quickly ended the conversation and moved on to speaking with the staff. Their employer reminded us, again, before letting us go to be discrete. She didn't want anyone suspecting anything.

I spoke with the cook first.

I hadn't seen the woman the evening before. By the time Andrew died in the kitchen, we were on to dessert, which had been baked well ahead of the dinner party. The cook had retired to her own home on the other side of town for the evening.

"I can't believe something like that happened in my kitchen." The woman pressed a hand to her large bosom and shook her head. "I've been cooking for Mr. Perring for years. He never complained about my cooking, even when he complained about everything else."

"Was he difficult to get along with?" I asked.

"He could be," she admitted, voice soft. "He drank, often to excess, and it could make him combative. I often warned the rest of the staff to ignore him when he got that way. It was easier to let him burn off the energy than to engage. That is what Nora was doing when he...when he..."

"Yes, he died only a few feet away from her," Sherborne said. "I suspect that is why she is not at work today?"

"It was too difficult for her," the cook said. "She feels such guilt, and I can only imagine. I wasn't even there, and I feel badly about my role. If I hadn't taught her to ignore him, perhaps something could have been done to save him. Nora said she heard banging noises and grumbles coming from the pantry, but she thought he was simply drunk and searching for more drink as he was prone to do. She couldn't have known what was really happening."

Like Mrs. Holworthy, the cook spoke of Andrew's struggles with drink and gambling. She said he came and went at all hours, and Mrs. Holworthy did her best to stop him.

"The two of them fought constantly," she said. "Mrs. Holworthy was concerned with the way Mr. Perring was raising the girls, and it's easy to understand why. The girls idolized their father, and the older they got, the more they were understanding his lifestyle. As children often do, they had a lot of questions, and Mrs. Holworthy didn't want them to learn the truth. She wanted her son-in-law to set himself straight. Unfortunately, he won't have the opportunity now."

Her chin dimpled, wagging as her eyes filled with tears.

"Did anything unusual happen prior to his death?" I asked. "Did you notice anything strange in the days leading up to the dinner party?"

"The fire was the most excitement we'd had around here for a very long time," she said.

"And Andrew wasn't here the day of the fire?"

She shook her head. "No. It was just Mrs. Holworthy, the girls, and Stephen, the driver. Though, he lives in the old carriage house out back. He never comes into the main house. Even Nora had been sent home early, which was quite unusual."

"Was it?"

"Oh, yes," she said. "Mrs. Holworthy is a fair

employer, and she is a very economical woman. We are all meant to work for every hour we are paid, nothing more or less. It was nearly a tragic coincidence that the day of the fire, she sent Nora away. If Nora had been here, she almost certainly would have caught the fire before it spread."

I frowned. "You know how the fire started?"

"A candle on the hallway table," she said.

"A candle?" I interrupted.

"The house's electric lighting has been unreliable of late, so we keep a few candles about for emergencies," she explained. "This one was sitting on a lace doily, and it burnt to the end and caught flame. No one is certain who left it there—the candle didn't match any of the other candles in the house—but when I came home from doing the weekly shopping, I smelled the smoke and was able to put out the flames with a rug before they could catch the wall."

"You are very brave," Sherborne said.

The cook gave him a shy smile. "We are all capable of extraordinary things in the right circumstances. I'm not special. I simply did what anyone would have done."

No one else on staff had anything else to add to the story. They all confirmed that Mrs. Holworthy and Andrew Perring had a tumultuous relationship, but I'd witnessed that myself at the dinner party. They also all confirmed that aside from Andrew and the girls, Ivy, and Robert Wade, Mrs. Holworthy didn't have any other guests or visitors the day of the fire or the days leading up to it. Meaning, that if Mrs. Holworthy's life really was in danger, one of those people would be responsible.

"It could be one of the servants," Sherborne suggested as we left.

"Possibly, but I don't know who it would be," I admitted. "None of them have the motive, and they all seem to respect their employer."

"Even if she is overbearing and judgmental," he added under his breath.

"Knowing what you want and asking for it isn't being overbearing."

Sherborne raised a brow, challenging me to defend my point, and I sighed.

"My Aunt Sarah has gone through the same thing for years. After her husband died, she inherited a great deal of money, and suddenly, everyone had opinions on how she treated everyone. They wanted her to be kind and soft-spoken and easygoing. Instead, she stands up for herself and has built a life for herself without anyone else's help, and I admire her for that."

He tugged his coat closer around his shoulders and shoved his hands in his pockets. "You keep saying that."

"What?"

"That you aren't in need of anyone's help."

"I'm not talking about myself right now. I'm talking about Mrs. Holworthy and—"

Sherborne grabbed my hand suddenly and pulled me to a stop. I hadn't even realized he'd removed his hand from his pocket. "Mrs. Holworthy is alone because her family is dead. Her life has been filled with tragedy and it left her alone and jaded; she didn't have another choice. You have a choice, Alice. You don't have to do everything alone. You can let people help you."

My heart thundered in my chest, and I wasn't sure why. "I know."

"Do you?"

I pulled my hand out of his and folded it behind my back. "Yes, you are helping me right now. With this case."

Sherborne nodded, but his mouth was still pulled down in a frown. When he dropped me at home, he gave me a silent nod in parting and left. I walked inside alone.

8

I wrote and sent Ivy Holworthy a message as soon as Sherborne left, and then waited all afternoon and into the next morning for her response. It was a short note, speaking of nothing beyond my condolences and a desire to see her. *It concerns your great aunt,* I added in hopes Ivy would realize the meeting was important and agree to it. Otherwise, I was afraid she'd ignore the note in favor of focusing on the loss her family had just suffered.

As morning gave way to midday, I worried that was precisely what had happened. I could have tried telephoning her next but the matter seemed too sensitive for something so impersonal. So, I decided to call on her myself.

Catherine and Hazel were playing in the living room when I left. Hazel had just mastered sitting upright, and everyone was fascinated with watching her hold herself up. Though I'd never been particularly fond of children

the way Catherine was, even I had to admit it was quite
the impressive feat.

"Auntie Alice is off again," Catherine said, grabbing
Hazel's little hand and lifting it in a wave. "Say bye-bye to
Auntie Alice."

I blew my niece a kiss, pulled on my coat, and left.

I considered going to visit Ivy on my own. If she was
anything like her great aunt, she might prefer speaking to
me alone rather than with Sherborne Sharp present.
Despite his seemingly unending charms, he didn't have
much sway with the Holworthy women. However, I
couldn't get Sherborne's words from the day before out of
my head.

I knew how to accept help. In fact, Sherborne had
helped me on several cases before. He'd come in at the
last moment to save my life on multiple occasions.
Though, admittedly, he'd had to do that because I'd gone
into those situations on my own.

Still, it wasn't like I wanted to go through life alone. I
just liked the idea of not relying on anyone. Of being able
to take care of myself and sort out my own problems.
Also, when I only had to worry about myself, life opened
up before me. If I'd had a husband and a child like
Catherine, I never could have rushed off to New York City
to spend a few weeks with my Aunt Sarah. I couldn't have
hurried off again to Yorkshire to see Catherine in her
time of need. My entire life, it was assumed—and in the
case of my mother, explicitly encouraged—that I would
grow older and marry, but I only wanted to grow older.
Rather than settle down with a husband and have children, I imagined being able to go wherever I wanted,
being able to do whatever I wanted. All of the doors that

had been closed to me as a child would be open once I was an adult, and marriage seemed like it would once again slam those doors shut.

So, I found myself standing in front of Sherborne's house.

It was a small flat in a rundown area, but his door and porch were spotlessly cleaned. When he opened the door, he looked ready to go in pinstripe trousers and suspenders. Except, he didn't have shoes on. Instead, he wore pale green socks. I was staring transfixed at his socks when Sherborne cleared his throat.

"Alice?" he asked. "What are you doing here?"

I shook my head and stood tall, folding my hands behind my back. "I came to see if you had the time and desire to accompany me to Ivy Holworthy's home today."

I couldn't be sure, but it almost seemed as though a flicker of disappointment flashed on his face. He covered it quickly, though, with a polite smile and nod. "Give me just a moment."

Less than a minute later, he reappeared with a pair of worn leather shoes, a jacket that matched his trousers, and a fedora.

"She isn't expecting us," I said quietly, glancing at the cab driver in the rearview mirror. He kept his eyes solely focused on the road, thought I couldn't help but feel as if he was listening in on our conversation. Even though I didn't expect the driver to know Mrs. Holworthy or anyone we were discussing, I still thought it would be best to be cautious. "I sent her a note yesterday, but she never responded."

"So, we are simply hoping she'll be at home?"

I nodded. "And willing to speak with us."

I instructed the driver to pull along the curb at the end of the block. I wanted a few minutes to talk strategy with Sherborne before we approached.

"I'll probably let you handle the conversation," Sherborne said before I could say anything. "If Ivy is anything like Mrs. Holworthy, she'd prefer I didn't say anything at all."

I bit back a smile. "I was going to suggest the same thing."

"Great minds think alike," he said, raising an eyebrow in a way that forced me to acknowledge the sharp planes of his face and the pleasantness of his smile. I pushed the thought away and started down the sidewalk. However, as soon as I did, the door to one of the flats opened, and Ivy herself walked onto the stoop.

She had on a vibrant yellow dress with a brown coat over the top that cinched in at her waist. Her heels were high with thin straps around her ankles, and her hair was pinned back in careful curls. She looked ready for an evening on the town, but it was barely mid-day.

I grabbed Sherborne's arm and yanked him behind a set of stairs. He yelped in surprise, but it was a low noise no one else was likely to hear.

"Ivy just came out of her house," I said in a harsh whisper.

He stared at me with wide eyes as though I had gone mad. "So? Aren't we going to speak with her? What does it matter if she sees us?"

Warmth flooded into my face. It didn't matter. He was right. Apparently, I'd grown accustomed to sneaking around and forgotten what it felt like to gather clues in the usual way—by interviewing suspects.

"She is leaving her home, and if we approach her now, she'll send us away," I justified.

Sherborne didn't look convinced as he stood to his full height and pulled on his suit jacket to straighten it. "Should we wait here or—?"

"We should follow her," I said.

Again, he stared at me, but I didn't want to explain anymore. He was here to help me, not hinder me, and Ivy was walking at a quick pace down the sidewalk. I didn't want to lose her. I looped my arm around his, laid my other hand on his forearm, and began a rather brisk, hopefully inconspicuous, walk.

Ivy lived on a popular street. People sat on their porches or pushed delicate prams down the sidewalk. It was an area full of young people, close to the university and restaurants and shops. It was a fashionable spot— one I wouldn't hate to see myself living in sooner rather than later, though my mother would balk at the idea, I was sure.

"Why are we following her?" Sherborne finally asked. "We only came to speak with her."

"And we will have more to talk about once we know where she is going."

He sighed but didn't argue, probably because he knew I made a fair point.

Aside from the fact that Ivy was Mrs. Holworthy's grandniece, we didn't know much else about the girl. Seeing how she spent her time would give me a way to form a connection with her and convince her to trust me —a virtual stranger—if nothing else.

Sherborne and I moved down the street, dodging past a mother and her young child who was crying over a scraped knee, never once taking our eyes from Ivy Holworthy.

At the end of the street, she took a left, heading towards the main road. I knew if we didn't make up ground soon, she'd outpace us and be lost in one of the shops or in the crowd of people on the busier street. So, the moment she had rounded the corner, I tugged on Sherborne's arm and began to run.

"Alice," he protested. "This all feels very unnecessary."

"I'm sure Mrs. Holworthy would be pleased to hear you think so. It would give her great confidence in your devotion to this case."

"It's Ivy," he said, as though that was reason enough. "She is a quiet girl who only wants to please her aunt. I do not believe she could be responsible for something as horrible as—"

When we turned the corner, Ivy was gone.

The stretch between the two roads was too wide for her to have already reached the other corner. Unless, of course, she'd been running.

Had she spotted us following her? If so, why would she run? Surely that would be a sign of guilt, wouldn't it?

"Where did she go?" I mumbled to myself, jerking Sherborne every which way as I turned in all directions.

"Oh." It was a short, startled sound. When I looked up, Sherborne was staring straight ahead, at the opposite side of the street, his mouth hanging open.

"What is it?" I asked, following his gaze. Though, by the time my eyes reached the destination, I knew exactly what he was looking at.

Ivy had not spotted us and run away to hide in the

crowds of the main road. She hadn't been going to the main road at all. Instead, she was in an alley across the street, and she was not alone.

A man, nearly a head taller than Ivy, with bright blonde hair sticking out from under his bowler hat stood in front of her. *Directly* in front of her.

They were standing together at the edge of the alley, blending in with the shadows, and he had his arms around her waist. Their heads were dipped low, foreheads touching.

"Who is that?" I whispered, although we were certainly far enough away that Ivy couldn't hear me, even if I'd spoken at normal volume.

"A man."

I sighed. "Obviously, but who? Ivy said she was unattached. Mrs. Holworthy was very proud of that."

"And Andrew Perring mentioned that she was lying."

I'd nearly forgotten about that. Andrew had been heavily intoxicated, and I'd taken most of his mutterings as nothing more than the nonsense of a drunk man. But could it have been more than that? Had he been close to revealing secrets of those at the table?

Giving even more credence to the theory, the blonde-haired man leaned forward and pressed his lips to Ivy's. It was a chaste kiss, an innocent brushing of lips, but it still felt deeply scandalous.

Suddenly, the two lovers touched noses, and then the man spun away, descending deeper into the alley, and Ivy walked back onto the street. She looked up and down the street to be sure no one had seen her, and I quickly grabbed Sherborne and turned him around so we were facing the wall.

"Yes, this is better," he mumbled. "Now, we are two strangers staring directly at a wall."

I looked over my shoulder and watched Ivy move back in the direction she'd come, back towards her house.

"She is going home. We should walk around the block and meet her coming from the other way."

If Sherborne disagreed with my plan or had other remarks, he kept them to himself, and I was grateful. On one hand, it was nice to have someone with me on this adventure, available to bear witness to what I saw and provide alternative viewpoints. On the other, he was being fussier than baby Hazel after a feeding.

We walked through the midday crowds of people searching out lunch or peering into shop windows, turned onto the side road, and then crossed the street and moved left towards Ivy's house.

She was no longer outside, so we mounted the stone steps and lifted her metal door knocker.

Ivy came to the door, a broad smile spread across her face and slightly out of breath. Then, she realized who we were and frowned. "Oh."

I laughed warmly. "I'm sorry. Were you expecting someone else? We shouldn't have come unannounced."

Ivy remembered her manners all at once and returned my smile. "No, I wasn't. I'm sorry, forgive me. I just didn't expect to see either of you...ever again, if I'm being honest."

"Honesty is preferred," Sherborne said, a twinkle in his eye that only I noticed.

She'd taken off her coat already, and I could now see the fluttering sleeves of the dress as well as the matching fabric belt around her waist with what appeared to be a crystal clasp on the buckle. Compared to Ivy, my simple skirt and blouse was a laughable attempt at an outfit.

"I wrote to you yesterday, but I'm sure you've been busy," I said. "With what happened at Mrs. Holworthy's and everything."

Ivy nodded quickly. "Right. Yes. It has been a strange time. I haven't been keeping up with my correspondence as well as I should be. Is that why you are here? To pay condolences?"

"In a way." I peered around her ever so slightly, looking through her front door. "Might we come in and—"

Ivy pressed a hand to her chest and gasped. "I'm so sorry. I've forgotten all sense of manners. Yes. Please, come in. May I get you anything?"

We both refused her offer and followed her through a narrow wooden entryway into a comfortable sitting room.

The furniture was outfitted in a bright floral pattern, arranged around a fireplace with a sturdy wooden mantle in the center. On top of it hung a portrait of Ivy as a much younger girl. She held a bouquet of white flowers in her lap.

"My aunt had that commissioned for my thirteenth birthday," Ivy said. "Or, my great-aunt, I should say."

"The two of you are close, aren't you?"

Ivy nodded. "We have been ever since my own grandparents died. Aunt Sarah has been like a grandmother to me for as long as I can remember. She is an outspoken woman, but quite caring."

"I have an Aunt Sarah myself who is very similar," I

said. "She lives on her own in New York City, and I do believe she could rule the world if she wanted."

Ivy smiled in understanding and then extended an arm for the two of us to take a seat on the sofa. She sat in the chair opposite, poised on the very edge as though ready to stand up at the shortest possible notice.

"I'm sure you're wondering why we came, and I want to be honest with you," I said.

Ivy's brows pinched together, concern wrinkling her forehead.

"Your aunt has asked us to look into the death of Andrew Perring," I finished.

It was not entirely honest, but it was more honest than I'd been with anyone else thus far. Ivy did not need to know that Mrs. Holworthy believed her life was at risk, but I could tell Ivy would be more willing to talk with us if she believed it was official business related to her aunt. If she thought I'd come here on my own, she wouldn't speak a word. But if there was a chance this conversation could be reported directly back to her aunt? She would be on her best behavior.

"Are the two of you detectives?"

"No," I said. At the same time, Sherborne nodded. "Of a sort."

"We have experience in that area," I clarified. "And since we were present the night of the death, your aunt wanted us to speak to the people who were there so we could have a better understanding of what occurred that night."

"I know I was in the powder room when Arthur died, but I didn't do anything wrong. There isn't even a direct access between the hallway and the kitchen. To get into the pantry, I would have had to crawl out a window and go through the back door, but Nora would have seen me if I'd done that. There isn't any possible way I could have—"

"Ivy," I said, overwhelmed by the speed at which words were pouring from the girl's mouth. "We are not here to accuse you of being a murderer."

Ivy's chest heaved as she looked from me to Sherborne and back again. "You aren't?"

"No. Of course, not. We just want to talk about what you know of Andrew Perring."

Ivy's shoulders fell, but her face was still flushed. "I'm afraid I don't know much. Andrew and I never spent much time together."

"Surely Mrs. Holworthy spoke to you about Andrew on occasion," Sherborne pressed. "You said you and she were close, did you not?"

"We are," Ivy said, a hint of defensiveness in her voice. "But speaking of Andrew made Aunt Sarah upset, so I avoided the topic. I tried to be sure our interactions were always uplifting."

"What did those interactions usually involve?"

"Conversation," she said. "Aunt Sarah liked to keep up with my education and social life. Also, I would spend time with my little cousins. Lucille would come with me on walks from time to time. The other girls were too young to be interested in such things, so we would sing songs, and I'd read to them."

"You are a kind cousin. Most young women wouldn't want to spend so much of their time with children," I said.

"I love children," Ivy admitted eagerly. "I've always

loved children, and I look forward to having my own someday."

I wondered what Mrs. Holworthy would think about that. She did not seem to be the kind of woman who encouraged such a traditional path for the women under her tutelage.

"Anyway, Aunt Sarah has given so much to me that I like to give back to her whenever possible," Ivy said. "When Anna died, Aunt Sarah became worried about the girls having a strong feminine presence in their life, so I agreed to meet with them often to try and encourage them in the ways they should go."

"Isn't that usually the concern of a parent?" I asked.

"Usually," Ivy said, her upper lip stiffening. "Anna worried about such things, but Andrew didn't. Especially not once Anna died. He hardly cared for the girls at all. As I already said, I did not know him well but that is because I did not want to know him. He was not a pleasant man."

Sherborne hummed in agreement. "I only knew him for a few short hours, and he made a rather...negative impression."

Ivy's eyes fluttered closed, and she shook her head. "It is shameful that those were his last moments on earth— drunk at a dinner party. I went by to see the girls yesterday afternoon, and they can barely understand what is happening. It is heartbreaking."

"It is," I agreed. "And I hate to make this time worse on any of you, but do you know of anyone who might have been angry with Andrew? Anyone who might have wanted to hurt him?"

Ivy blinked, her eyes going wide. "I can't imagine

anyone I know—least of all anyone at that party—doing something so heinous as to kill a man, however..."

"Yes?" I prompted after she went quiet.

"Well, I did overhear a loud discussion between Andrew and Mr. Wade just a few weeks ago," Ivy said, pressing her lips together self-consciously.

"Do you mean an argument?" Sherborne asked.

She nodded. "Aunt Sarah was out for the day, and I was spending time with the girls. I came downstairs to get Pearl's favorite blanket, which she was always leaving all over the house, and I heard voices coming from the sitting room. I approached and recognized Andrew's voice first. He said that he would tell Aunt Sarah everything if Robert didn't. I'm not sure what he meant by that, neither of them elaborated."

"What did Robert Wade say?"

"He was upset," she said. "Very emotional. He said he would sooner die than hurt my Aunt Sarah that way."

Sherborne and I exchanged a look.

"But he couldn't have," Ivy said quickly. "Robert has always been a gentle man. A kind man. He has been such a good friend to my Aunt Sarah, and he would never hurt someone she cared for."

"And did she care for Andrew Perring?" Sherborne asked.

Ivy looked down at the floor and chewed on her lower lip. "In her own way, yes. He was the father of her grandchildren, and she loves her grandchildren more than anything. They are the only family she has."

"She has you, too," I said.

Ivy smiled at my kindness. "She has given me a

wonderful life. She wants what is best for me, and I have tried to repay her kindness in every way I can."

"You've said that already." Sherborne's tone was teasing, but his eyes were focused, assessing Ivy's reaction. "How exactly do you repay her kindness?"

"By following the simple rules she has given me," Ivy said with a smile.

"Which are?"

"She wants me to focus on my education."

"Which means you are not to have any male suitors?" I asked, stating explicitly what Ivy seemed to only want to hint at.

She nodded.

"I can't imagine that is easy for a beautiful girl such as yourself," Sherborne said.

Ivy smiled at Sherborne, and I felt a strange emotion curl in my stomach. She was lovely. Anyone with eyes could see that. Still, I didn't think it appropriate that Sherborne comment on it. We were interviewing her, not seducing her.

"I'm so busy between school and my family that it is easy enough," Ivy said with the same easy tone in which she'd said everything else. "Besides, my education depends upon it. If Aunt Sarah discovered I was seeing anyone, she wouldn't agree to pay for my schooling. That is added motivation to follow her rules."

We thanked Ivy for her time and left a few minutes later. The moment we were out of earshot, Sherborne sighed. "We can't trust a word she said that entire interview."

"She did lie with relative ease," I admitted. "The topic

of romance didn't even seem to make her uncomfortable. Apparently, she is very practiced in the art of deception."

"What now?"

"Whether she was lying or not, there seems only one logical place to go next," I said. "It's time we talk to Robert Wade."

9

I sent our maid, Bessie, with a note for Mrs. Holworthy, requesting a meeting with her and Robert Wade. Mrs. Holworthy had made it clear she didn't suspect Robert Wade, but if Ivy was telling the truth about the argument she'd overheard between Robert and Andrew, then it would be negligence not to look into it. What could be so bad that Mr. Wade would rather die than Mrs. Holworthy discover it? And had he, instead, decided he'd rather kill the person who knew than kill himself?

"Sherborne could have stayed for lunch," Catherine said. "He rushed off before I could say hello."

"He had other matters to attend to," I said, though I knew no such thing. Truthfully, I knew it would have been polite to invite him to lunch, and he likely would have accepted the offer. But I did not want Sherborne to spend more time with my family.

Despite my constant assurances that there was nothing going on between Sherborne and myself beyond our working relationship, I could see that Catherine suspected otherwise. The more time Sherborne spent in the company of my family, the more attached Catherine would become to the notion that he and I were together, and I was not sure that was a good idea.

Catherine spooned a bite of something mushy into Hazel's mouth, swiping the spoon across her bottom lip to keep it from dribbling down her chin, and sighed. "That is too bad. When Charles arrives, I'm sure he'll want to see Sherborne. The two of them got along well when he came to Yorkshire."

"Mr. Sharp was in Yorkshire?" Papa asked, showing an unusual amount of interest in the lunchtime conversation.

"Briefly," I said. "He only came for a day and a night."

"To see Alice," Catherine added.

Papa frowned. "Why is it I am only now hearing about this?"

"We spoke about it at length just the other day," Mama said. "You were sitting right where you are now with your paper."

His mustache twitched. "I just think I ought to know when my daughter is seeing a man. That is any father's right."

"It is not," I said sharply.

Everyone turned to me, and I swallowed down my frustration. "I mean that I am not *seeing* anyone. Mr. Sharp is assisting me with a case."

"A case?" Papa asked, looking from me to my mother, confusion written in the lines of his forehead. "What sort of case?"

Mama quickly filled him in on the preceding days'

events, and his perplexed expression remained fixed until she was done.

"You are solving crimes?" he asked.

"Not officially, but yes," I admitted. "I have been for a little while now."

His lips opened and closed, words failing him. "I'm not sure...I didn't realize...when did—"

Before he could form an entire thought, the door opened, and Bessie came bustling into the room. She must have just returned from her outdoor errand, for her cheeks were still pink from the chill.

"Miss Beckingham?"

Catherine started to turn before she remembered that was no longer her name.

"Yes?"

"I left your letter with Mrs. Holworthy's maid, but before I could even make it down the steps, the lady herself was there. She asked to see you immediately."

"Immediately?"

Bessie nodded. "It seemed urgent, Miss."

I thanked her for her assistance and asked her to send for our driver, George.

When I pushed away from the table, Papa slid his chair back as well. He moved to stand up, but then sat back in his chair. "You are going right now? In the middle of lunch?"

"I'm sorry," I said. "I know it is rude, but I have eaten my fill, and I must speak with my client."

"I'm not sure how I feel about you going," Papa said. He was a quiet man. When he did exhibit an emotion— especially in the years since Edward's crimes and death— it was usually frustration or disappointment. He loved us all, and I knew that, but he rarely felt the need to show it. Instead, he busied himself with business and news while Mama handled the household and family affairs. "I don't think it is safe for a young lady like you to be involved in such grim affairs. It isn't right."

I smoothed down my skirt and pushed my chair back into the table. "I appreciate your concern. Truly, I do. Unfortunately, it is not your decision to make."

He opened his mouth to respond, but I backed away from the table with a wave. "I'm a grown woman, and it is time for me to make my own decisions."

"Grown woman," Papa said with a shake of his head.

"I am." I spoke clearly, doing my best to keep my voice soft and even. "I respect all of you so much, but the time for you to tell me how to live my life has passed. If you have more to say, it can be discussed later. Right now, I must go."

Without another word, I turned and walked out of the dining room. George would probably already be waiting outside, so I opened the front door and strode out of the house with my head held high.

"Thank you for coming so promptly," Mrs. Holworthy said, her wrinkled hands clutching a cup of tea. She gave me a warm smile, but the expression faded as her gaze shifted to Sherborne. He stiffened next to me. I nearly smiled at his obvious discomfort in the face of this old woman.

"Of course. We wanted to speak with you anyway—

which you know since you received my note this morning, I'm sure."

"I did," she said. "That is why I've asked you to come. Not because you requested my presence, but because I'd like to speak to you about the...changing nature of this investigation."

I frowned. "I'm not sure I understand your meaning."

"Police detectives came by the house again this morning, and they believe Andrew's death was caused by a poisoning of some kind," she said. "They think due to excessive alcohol consumption."

"Is that what you think?" I asked.

Mrs. Holworthy pursed her lips and leaned back in her chair, adjusting the many layers of her forest green dress and sweater. "I believe Andrew was poisoned, but I do not believe it was an accident."

Sherborne and I both sat forward in our seats.

"I agree," I said quickly. "That is why I sent that letter to you this morning. I've uncovered some interesting information that has led me to the belief that—"

"Andrew poisoned himself."

The words died in my throat. "Excuse me?"

"I believed my life was in danger, and I'm still confident in that. I believe my life was in danger from Andrew. As you mentioned before, he would have inherited a good deal of money from my death, and I think he grew tired of waiting. I had recently cut back how much money I provided him for the care of the children, and that interfered with his ability to gamble and drink as he liked. So, he sought to kill me with poison, but he was so drunk he poisoned himself instead."

That was certainly a theory. A possible one, but it did

not line up with the information we'd learned from Ivy Holworthy. If she'd been telling the truth then Robert Wade had a motive for wanting Andrew Perring out of the picture, and I needed to figure out what it was.

"You believe Andrew set the fire outside of your sitting room, as well?" Sherborne asked.

"He was the only person in the house unaccounted for," Mrs. Holworthy said. "He left the house that morning and did not return until much later in the day. Even when he did, he showed very little concern for my welfare. I wasn't injured at all, but I would have expected him to be worried about me. Instead, he spent the entire evening upstairs."

"With his daughters?" It was clear by the tone in Sherborne's voice what his question was really saying, and Mrs. Holworthy narrowed her eyes.

"The girls only learned about the fire after the fact. They were hardly traumatized by it. I was the one who had been in harm's way."

I moved to the very edge of the sofa, positioning myself between Mrs. Holworthy and Sherborne to the degree possible. "Your theory is a valid one, and we will certainly look into it, but we uncovered new information this morning. That information is the reason I reached out to you. I hoped to ask you about the relationship between Andrew Perring and Robert—"

"Robert is here, actually," Mrs. Holworthy said, raising her voice. "Robert?"

Just then, the man himself appeared in the doorway to the sitting room, a plain, curious smile on his face. "Did you need me?"

She waved him in, and he took up position in the

chair next to Mrs. Holworthy's. "I don't want to intrude on your conversation."

"It actually involves you," Mrs. Holworthy said. "I believe Alice wanted to ask you a few questions."

I looked to Mrs. Holworthy, trying to determine what exactly I was allowed to say. Last I'd known, I was not supposed to let anyone know about the attempts on her life lest the killer's efforts increase. And especially now that I believed Robert Wade could be the main suspect in a murder, I didn't want to say anything that could put her in danger.

Even if Robert's anger had been with Andrew, it seemed that anger involved something in his relationship with Mrs. Holworthy. Perhaps, Robert hoped to kill Andrew and inherit a larger sum of money. Though, with Andrew's three daughters still alive, that seemed unlikely.

Even without the motive of money, Robert could have killed Andrew just to keep him quiet. In which case, my bringing up the argument now could make Mrs. Holworthy aware of a truth that could put her in even greater danger than she was before. However I proceeded, I had to do so carefully.

"Say whatever you would like," Mrs. Holworthy said, reading the question in my eyes. "Robert knows everything."

"Everything?" Sherborne asked.

Robert nodded. "Sarah finally told me today she suspected her life was in danger, and I could not believe she waited so long to inform me. I would have been here night and day to protect her had I known. The idea that Andrew nearly carried his plan through makes me ill. I can't imagine what the world would be without Sarah Holworthy in it."

"If I'd felt I needed protection, I would have reached out. However, I am perfectly capable of taking care of myself." Her voice was stern, but still, she reached over and patted his hand where it rested on the arm of the chair. The gesture was familiar and warm, and it was hard to imagine any ill will could exist between the two friends. Though, according to Ivy, a secret lay between them.

"What did you wish to speak to me about?" Mr. Wade asked, turning back to us. "I am more than happy to offer whatever help I can to the two of you."

"Well," I said, suddenly uncomfortable. I had planned to confront Mr. Wade about his supposed argument with Andrew Perring, but not in front of Mrs. Holworthy. Not moments after the two of them had announced that they were in cahoots with one another.

Sherborne's hand ever so lightly touched my back, and then he began to speak. "I heard from a reliable source that you and Mr. Perring engaged in a heated conversation only a couple of weeks ago."

Normally, I'd bristle at someone taking the lead on my investigation, but Sherborne had done so because he could see that I was uncomfortable. I was suddenly grateful to have a partner.

Mrs. Holworthy's gaze sharpened on Sherborne, but she didn't say anything. She simply turned to Robert Wade and awaited his response.

Robert smiled, though the expression was thin. His throat bobbed. "Your source is correct. Andrew and I exchanged words."

"In regards to what?" Mrs. Holworthy asked, looking shocked by the revelation.

Mr. Wade lowered his chin and gave Mrs. Holworthy a small smile. "You, my dear."

"You and Andrew argued about Mrs. Holworthy?" Sherborne asked.

Robert Wade unwillingly dragged his eyes from his friend and nodded. "As was evident at the dinner party the night of his death, Andrew did not treat his mother-in-law with the respect her station and kindness deserved. She cared for him and his children, yet he spoke poorly of her at every turn and sought out ways to purposefully make her life more difficult."

"Through his drinking and gambling?" I asked.

"Yes," Robert said. "But in other ways, too. He always claimed to have secret information on her friends and family, information that could destroy relationships if there was any truth to it."

"And was there truth to it?"

"Never," Robert said with finality and a firm shake of his head. "As his behavior became more unchecked, he tried to ensure his main source of income wouldn't suddenly turn him out on the street."

"I never would have," Mrs. Holworthy interjected. "If only for the sake of those girls. I wouldn't have dreamed of separating them from their last living parent, and the idea of them being raised without the protection and security I offered…" Her voice trailed off, and she shook her head. "I don't even want to think on it."

"Your argument with him centered on his disrespect and these lies?" I asked, bringing the conversation back to the central focus.

Robert nodded. "It did. I told Andrew he should treat Mrs. Holworthy with more respect, and he became angry. He was also drunk at the time, as it turned out. Had I known how drunk, perhaps I would have waited to speak with him another time."

"When was this?" Mrs. Holworthy asked. "I don't recall any of this."

"I didn't mention it to you because it didn't seem worth mentioning. The conversation did not go at all how I hoped, and I didn't want to cause any more strife between the two of you than I already had," Robert said.

Sherborne cleared his throat, drawing all eyes to him. "Our source overheard you say that you would rather die than have Mrs. Holworthy find something out...any idea what they could be referring to?"

Sarah's eyes went wide, and she leaned slightly away from her friend, drawing her hand to her lap.

Robert blinked at Sherborne for a moment and then snapped his fingers as though just remembering something. "Ah, yes. Andrew claimed he had some proof of illegal business dealings on my end, and he would show Sarah if I didn't tell her myself. He claimed he could ruin my business from the inside out. All of it was lies, of course."

"Then why would you rather die than tell her?" I asked.

"Because I *would* rather die than hurt Sarah," Mr. Wade said, sending a small smile to his friend. "We had spoken to Andrew in the past about these lies and how they hurt Sarah, so I did not want her to know he was still telling them if it wasn't necessary. That is what I meant by that."

His explanation made sense, though I couldn't help but feel there was something too neat about it. Something that allowed Robert to escape without a single spot on his reputation, whereas Andrew played the role of the villain.

"You should have told me about this," Mrs. Holworthy said sternly. "Though, I'm glad to have the air clear now."

"As am I," Robert said. "I wish we could have had the opportunity to speak with Andrew about it ourselves and work things out, but unfortunately, that won't happen now."

"No," Mrs. Holworthy said sadly, looking at the floor reflectively for a moment. Then, she sat up and looked straight at me. "While we are on the subject of sad endings, I'm afraid our time together has come to an end, as well."

"Excuse me?"

Mrs. Holworthy lifted one shoulder in a shrug. "There hardly seems reason to continue on with this investigation when it is clear what happened."

"I wouldn't say it is clear," Sherborne said, looking to me for confirmation that I agreed with him.

"Your theory is a strong one, but there is no proof that Andrew was trying to kill you," I said. "The police believe Andrew was poisoned, but it could have been by anyone's hand, not necessarily his own. I think ending the search for answers now opens you up to potential dangers from—"

"From whom?" she asked pointedly, her words clipped and sharp. "You have been investigating for days and have found nothing more concrete than the police were able to find. I am sorry, but I don't see the value in paying more money for the same conclusion to be arrived at. I am a wealthy woman, but I do not waste money frivolously. And that is what I believe it would be to continue on with this case: frivolous."

"Respectfully, I disagree," I said, glancing in Robert Wade's direction. I wished he would leave so I could speak to Mrs. Holworthy plainly. "We have been taking this case slowly so as not to rouse suspicion amongst your friends and family, per your request, which means we have not yet investigated every angle of this case. There are still suspects remaining."

"I'm sorry, Miss Beckingham, but the time has come," she said, standing up and extending an arm towards me, ready to escort us to the door. "You did satisfactory work, and should the need ever arise again, I'll be sure to call on you. Until then, I hope you will be well."

It was clear Mrs. Holworthy's mind had been made up and there was nothing I could say to change it. So, I allowed myself to be herded to the door. "I hope you will be well, too. Truly, I do."

Mrs. Holworthy and Mr. Wade stood in the doorway, his figure standing just over her shoulder in the shadows of the entryway. Knowing what I knew, it was quite an ominous image.

"This is not how I expected this case to end," Sherborne said, tucking his arm around mine as we moved down the sidewalk. "I thought we would either discover the murderer or be able to tell Mrs. Holworthy there was nothing to fear. I certainly didn't think she would be the one to dismiss us."

If the matter had been about anything other than life and death, I would have walked away when asked. I would have respected the wishes of the client who hired me and gone on to the next case or whatever it was my future held. However, as it stood, a woman's life hung in the balance, and I could not in good conscience forget that. I said as much to Sherborne.

"What do you propose we do?" he asked.

"We?" I turned to him, eyebrow arched.

He frowned. "Of course. Do you think I would walk away?"

"From the start you have seemed to side with the authorities on the manner of Andrew's death. I thought this would be enough confirmation to convince you I was mad."

Sherborne stopped suddenly and grabbed me by the elbow, turning me towards him. The wind was cold, the ground shimmery from a rain earlier in the day, and no one else was on the street with us. We were alone.

"Alice, I have never in my life met anyone more reckless than you."

I frowned. "That isn't what I thought you were going to say."

He smiled and continued. "You rush headlong into danger, you don't listen to anyone once your mind is made up, and you see things I don't see. You listen and watch and observe the world closely. By all measures, you are mad."

"I'm confused."

"But you know what you are very rarely?" Sherborne leaned down so I could see the streaks of gold in his dark eyes. "Wrong. To my constant frustration, you are almost always right. So, even though I do not believe there is anything to this case, I must admit that if you think there is something strange going on, you are probably right."

My mouth curled into a smile, and I pressed my lips together to contain it. "That is very kind of you to say."

"I'm not being kind. I'm being honest."

I took a deep breath, trying to settle the nerves fluttering in my stomach.

Sherborne released my arm and stood back, rising up to his full height. "So, what next?"

"I say we do what Andrew Perring proposed the night of his murder—I suggest we find Robert Wade's briefcase and take a look inside."

10

I wanted to go directly to Robert Wade's home, especially since we knew he was at Mrs. Holworthy's house right now; however, we couldn't go in unarmed.

"You have a pistol?" Sherborne hissed.

"In the back of my closet, hidden inside of a..." I hesitated, face flushing. "Inside of an undergarment."

Sherborne rolled his neck uncomfortably. "Do you really think it is necessary?"

"I've gone into situations like this more times than I'd care to admit, and I know I do not want to go in unarmed. Whatever happens, I want to be able to defend myself. To defend you."

"You are a remarkable woman, Alice, but please, let me keep some of my dignity. At least let me pretend I would be the one protecting you."

I grinned and turned to tell him to wait outside for me while I ran up to my room. But before I could say anything, the front door to my house opened, and my father stepped out.

"I presume this is Mr. Sherborne Sharp?" His eyes were hooded, watchful.

Sherborne mounted the steps quickly and took my father's hand. "Yes, Lord Ashton."

"You've met him before, Papa," I said, rolling my eyes as I followed behind Sherborne. "He was at the house just the other day, but you were too busy with your paper."

"I'm not busy now," my father snapped. "And I'd like to speak with the gentleman you've been spending so much time with."

We did not have time for this at all, but I didn't see a way around it. For whatever reason, my father had suddenly taken an interest in my life, and if I was going to leave this house again today, I would have to play along. We would both have to.

"You two talk in the sitting room." I pushed Sherborne forward. "I need to run up to my room."

Just before walking into the sitting room, Sherborne looked over his shoulder at me, concern etched into the lines of his face. I shooed him forward, giving him a smile that I hoped conveyed how little he needed to be worried about this conversation.

After all, Catherine was engaged to Charles before either of my parents ever met the man. They couldn't be that worried about me. Mama knew Sherborne, and even if I knew he had a spotted past, my parents knew nothing about his thieving ways. By all appearances, he was a handsome, kind, respectable young man.

Now that I considered it, Sherborne simply was those

things. He didn't only appear handsome, kind, and respectable. He had proven himself over the length of our friendship—especially recently—to have a generous heart, concern for the wellbeing of others, and a mind that sought justice.

And perhaps most importantly to me, he supported my dreams. Sherborne did not tell me to settle down and do something suitable. Instead, he went along with me to assist in whatever ways he could. What kind of man would do something like that?

"He is in love with you."

I startled at the sudden voice and pressed my back against the wall, ready to fight off an attacker if necessary. Then, I saw my sister Catherine standing in the doorway to her room, a sleeping Hazel on her shoulder.

I pressed a hand to my heart. "You startled me, Catherine."

Catherine just tipped her head to the side and smiled. "That man down there is in love with you, and you know it as well as I do."

"I know no such thing," I said, walking past her to my room. I hoped she wouldn't follow, but she did.

"Why are you refusing to see what is plainly in front of you?" Catherine whispered, trying not to wake Hazel. "You've found someone willing to indulge you in your whims and—"

"Is that what you think this is?" I asked, spinning to face her. "A whim?"

"I didn't mean it—"

"It wasn't a whim when you asked me for help," I reminded her. "And it wasn't a whim when I discovered

Edward's murder was a plot carried out by our cousin Rose's older brother."

Catherine had been prepared to defend her comment, but then her face went blank. Her eyes widened, and she took a step back. "What are you saying?"

I'd never told anyone what I'd discovered in New York. It seemed pointless to dwell on it. Edward was gone regardless, and now, the man who killed him was gone, too. But I couldn't take it back now.

"Edward was working in tandem with a dangerous criminal, and he couldn't get himself untangled. That criminal was The Chess Master, Rose's older brother."

"And by Rose...you mean...?"

"Nellie Dennet's brother," I said. "When Edward was imprisoned, he became worried Edward would turn him in and reveal his identity, so he had him killed. It was all part of a plan."

Catherine blinked, stunned, and I reached out and laid a hand on her arm. "I'm sorry."

"No, I'm sorry," she said quickly, her voice soft. "I had no idea you were working to uncover any of that. I didn't realize..."

"I wasn't going to tell you," I admitted. "And please don't tell Mama and Papa. It would only hurt them."

She nodded and then sighed, a sad smile tipping the edge of her mouth up. "I suppose I can understand why love isn't at the forefront of your mind. You've been busy."

"A bit," I said with a wink. "In fact, I still am. Sherborne and I need to get out of this house quickly. An urgent matter has arisen, and we must deal with it before someone is hurt."

Catherine watched as I went into my room, dug into my closet, and returned with my pistol.

Her eyes widened, a protective hand cradling the back of Hazel's blonde head. Then, she nodded. "If it is a distraction you need, I can help. So long as you promise to tell me everything later."

"I swear it."

She grinned for a moment before her expression turned serious. "You go downstairs and stand near the front door. I'll create a distraction, and when Mama and Papa come running, you grab your man and go."

"He isn't my man."

Catherine rolled her eyes and waved me forward, towards the stairs.

I did exactly as Catherine asked. Papa and Sherborne were still in the sitting room, sitting opposite one another. I could see their profiles, but neither of them noticed me walk by.

"Alice is a bright girl, but I'm sure you've seen how headstrong she is," Papa said. "She gets these wild notions and won't be swayed against them. I gave up trying to convince her of anything long ago, which is why I'm talking to you now and not to her."

Catherine appeared at the top of the stairs, moving down them as silently as possible.

"Alice needs someone who can control her flights of fancy," Papa continued.

"I don't think Alice is capable of being controlled," Sherborne said. "Nor would I wish to do such a thing."

I smiled, glad no one could see me.

"I won't allow my daughter to be injured because she goes unchecked," Papa said sharply. "She needs a strong man, capable of directing her where she needs to go, and if that is not you then—"

"I can assure you right now it is not," Sherborne said plainly. "I respect your daughter too much to condescend to her and pretend I know what is best for her."

My father inhaled sharply, ready to launch into a speech of his own, but Sherborne continued.

"I care for her deeply and will always do my best to ensure she is safe, but I will not do that by locking her away like some prized bird. I've made that mistake before, and Alice made it clear to me that she would not permit that kind of behavior. Moreover, I've learned it is not necessary. Alice is a strong, intelligent woman, and if she chooses me to be by her side, I will be there with a grateful heart and full trust in her abilities to live a life of her own choosing. I hope you can respect that."

Whether my father could or could not respect Sherborne's opinion was lost to the sudden scream that came from the stairs.

I jolted, surprised by the sound, and turned to see Catherine lying at the bottom of the stairs with a crying Hazel pressed to her chest.

I was so overcome with worry that I nearly ran to Catherine myself, afraid she'd fallen, when she winked at me and then began to cry, loud sobs bursting out of her.

There was a commotion from the sitting room, and Papa burst out, horror written on his face.

"I slipped and fell," Catherine exclaimed. "I think Hazel is all right. Is she? Please take her."

Papa ran over to help Catherine, and then Sherborne appeared in the doorway. He was about to jump into action as well, but before he could, I grabbed his arm and pulled him to the door.

"Alice, wait," he said, tugging on my hold. "Your sister—"

"Is fine," I finished in a whisper, opening the front door. "It's a distraction so we can leave. Come on."

Sherborne looked back over his shoulder once and then followed me out of the house without another argument.

WE STOOD across the street from Robert Wade's house for several minutes, trying to decide if he was still at Mrs. Holworthy's house or if he had come home.

"No lights on inside," Sherborne said.

"We could see if there is a car parked in the back, though Mrs. Holworthy's home is close enough that he could have walked." I sighed. "Even if he is gone, there will be a member of staff inside, certainly."

"All right, may I formulate a plan?" Sherborne asked.

I frowned at him. "Of course, you may."

He raised a brow. "Usually it is you who is making the plans, so I had to be sure you would be receptive to mine."

"I am becoming less receptive by the second," I warned. "Out with it."

He smiled and continued. "My car is just around the corner. I can drive to Mrs. Holworthy's, observe whether Mr. Wade is still there or not, and then be back within ten minutes. You can remain here, watching to see if he returns while I am gone. Once I'm back, we'll have a better idea of how to proceed."

It did seem a practical, logical course of action. Though, I hated the idea of sitting and waiting for Sherborne to return.

"You can't possibly argue with such a simple plan. It's hardly a plan at all," Sherborne said. "More of a preamble to the plan."

Sherborne had been following my lead for days—months, really—and after the way he'd defended me to my father, I wanted him to know that I trusted him, as well.

"That sounds like a good idea," I said. "You go to Mrs. Holworthy's, and I will wait here for your arrival."

Sherborne looked momentarily stunned that I'd agreed with him, but he quickly regained his composure, made me promise I'd remain where I stood while he was gone, and then hurried around the corner to his car.

Standing still had never been a strong suit of mine. Ever since I was a child, I wiggled and stretched constantly, incapable of holding steady even for the length of a conversation. I'd become better at it over the years, a sense of propriety overriding my innate desire to be in constant motion. But standing across the street from Robert Wade's home, staring at the dark windows, beyond which a crucial clue could lie, felt like torture.

I might as well have been standing there for hours. It seemed impossible, but I felt as though I could see the sun moving towards the horizon, leeching the day of its light and warmth.

I'd promised Sherborne I would remain where I stood, and I intended to keep that promise. I wanted to prove to him that I could follow orders. I could respect plans he made just as he respected mine. And I really did want to do all of those things, but when the front door of Robert Wade's house opened, and the man himself walked onto the stoop, I forgot Sherborne Sharp entirely.

I darted to a shrub growing along the curb and hid behind it, watching through the sparse branches as Mr. Wade adjusted his hat and set off down the sidewalk at a fast clip. Wherever he was going, he seemed in a hurry to get there, and he had just turned the corner when I came out from my hiding place and darted across the street.

By the time Sherborne returned from Mrs. Holworthy's, Robert could be back from wherever he was going. The window of opportunity was now, and I intended to take it.

There was no fence around his front garden, so it was easy to walk onto his lawn and around the side of the house. I tested low windows as I passed, hoping to find one unlocked. Then, I reached the back of the house and found a door. Through the window set into the wood, I could see a modest and, more importantly, empty kitchen beyond. I turned the handle and, when it rotated in my hand, said a silent prayer of thanks.

The kitchen was warm, the remnants of a fire flickering in the stone fireplace, and I tip-toed across the tile floor and towards a swinging door that opened onto a hallway.

With every step, I expected someone to come running and catch me trespassing, but there was no movement anywhere in the house.

Rooms were set off the long hallway, a dining room on the right, a bathroom beyond that, and a sitting room at the far corner of the house nearest the street. On the left, there was a closet, a staircase to the upper floor, and then, tucked in front of the stairs near the front door was a heavy wooden door that had been left partially opened. One glance inside told me it was where I needed to be.

Bookshelves lined one wall and a map covered the other. It was a map of London with pinpricks all over it. A little investigating showed it was all the places where Robert Wade had real estate investments. It was his way of tracking them, apparently.

The desk was tidy, a bottle of ink sitting on one corner with a fountain pen, a heavy typewriter near a telephone at the other corner, and a stack of papers in the center, ready for Mr. Wade to scribble important notes upon them.

I rounded the desk and pulled on the drawers, but the top two were locked and the bottom one on the right was filled with nothing but more blank paper and envelopes. I searched the bookshelves and ran my hand along the underside of the desk in search of a key, but there was nothing.

Just as I was beginning to worry that Sherborne would arrive any moment and be waiting for me outside —just as I was beginning to despair that this had all been for naught—I looked down at the floor just underneath the desk and saw a leather briefcase.

The night of the dinner party, Andrew Perring had drunkenly asked Robert Wade to produce a briefcase and show us all his secrets. Could this be the same briefcase?

I grabbed the case and set it on the corner of the clean desk, trying to keep my expectations low. The case felt lighter than I would expect. Perhaps, it was empty. In all likelihood, anything scandalous would be hidden away in the locked drawers of Mr. Wade's desk, not in the briefcase under his desk. It was hidden from view, but still, it was accessible and unlocked. Likely, there would be nothing inside worth anything, and I would be forced to return to Sherborne, admit that I'd gone against his plan, and reveal that it had been for nothing anyway.

What would I do next if it turned out Robert Wade was not lying to Mrs. Holworthy? I knew Ivy was lying about having a gentleman friend, but that couldn't justify murder, could it? Even if her education was on the line.

I pushed the thoughts from my mind and opened the case.

Part of me expected to see nothing, but instead, there was a bundle of papers, strapped down to the lid with a buckled strap. I undid the buckle and released the pages.

The first page appeared to be from a ledger. On the left column was a large sum of money, in the center were deductions from that sum, and on the far right was the remaining difference. These numbers on the right were circled with a heavy hand. One-hundred pounds. Three-hundred and fifty pounds. Four-hundred and seventy-five pounds.

I flipped past the first page to the next and saw it was a letter addressed to Robert Wade.

MR. WADE,

YOU'VE MADE it no secret that you do not believe my mother-in-law, and your friend, should concern herself with my *finances any longer, and I wonder if you'd rather me suggest she concern herself with yours? I've included an overview of the large sums she has loaned you, though I've noted a few discrepancies. If we work together, perhaps we can discover where this money has disappeared to without concerning Sarah.*

YOUR FRIEND,
    Andrew Perring

I TURNED BACK to the ledger at the start and understood it all the more clearly now. Mrs. Holworthy had loaned Mr. Wade several sums of money, and he had invested it just as he'd claimed—though, not all of it. Some of the money was unaccounted for, and Andrew knew.

The conversation Ivy had overheard that day at her aunt's home had not been Mr. Wade being concerned for Mrs. Holworthy's feelings. Rather, he'd been concerned with her wrath. He was worried what would happen to his business and reputation if his long-time friend learned he'd been stealing from her.

Could that have led him to remove Andrew from the picture entirely?

It was not proof, but it was reason enough to bring the information to Mrs. Holworthy and alert her that her friend may not be as trustworthy as she hoped.

I folded the papers and tucked them into the waist-band of my skirt just beneath my blouse. Just as I finished, I heard a noise in the hallway. Footsteps moving across the hardwood floor.

My heart stopped.

I'd been so focused on the documents that I'd forgotten where I was. I'd forgotten the danger I was in.

The footsteps moved closer, and I knew there was no way out. I would not be able to reach the window, open it, and climb out safely before whoever was approaching found me. So, when the footsteps were just outside the door, I dropped to the floor and hid behind the desk.

I prayed the person was going up the stairs rather than into the study, but the hinges on the door squeaked as it opened. I could feel my heartbeat in every part of my body.

I leaned forward to look under the desk and could see short black heels tapping across the floor. That was some comfort. It was not Robert Wade himself. Still, the servant moved slowly around the edge of the room, humming as she went, and I surmised she was dusting the bookshelves.

Where was Sherborne? Was he outside? Even if he was, he couldn't know I needed his help. I would be on my own to solve this problem, and there seemed no delicate way to do it. Soon enough, she would come around the desk, and I would have nowhere to hide.

I had the pistol still strapped to my side, but I wouldn't harm an innocent housemaid. Surprise would have to be my saving grace.

Steeling myself with a quiet, shallow breath, I touched where the papers were tucked beneath my waistband and, certain they were secure, I bolted to my feet, propelling myself forward.

Everything happened at once.

I clattered clumsily across the floor, rushing for the

door, and the maid screamed, slamming her back against the bookshelves.

I didn't even look at her as I ran out the door and into the hallway.

"Stop!" the maid screamed behind me. "Help!"

A voice responded from somewhere deep in the house, but I didn't remain to see who it was. Instead, I ran down the hallway, through the kitchen, and out the door.

Just as there was no fence in the front, there was no fence in the back. I cut through Mr. Wade's back garden and the back gardens of his neighbors. Then, I followed a narrow alleyway down to the sidewalk, and turned right, still running at full speed.

11

I didn't know how long I ran, but I kept going until my legs shook with every step and my lungs felt as though they would burst. I ran until I knew I was far enough away to have not been followed. And only when I stopped, leaning back against a lamppost to catch my breath, did I remember Sherborne.

Was he still waiting for me outside of Mr. Wade's home? I could go back to see, but I would risk being recognized by the household staff, who were all probably on high alert after my daring escape.

Would Sherborne's presence on the street be suspicious? Would he be thought to be working with the female intruder?

Too many questions to consider crossed my mind, and I decided the best course of action would be to go to my parents' home and send George around to tell Sherborne what had happened. Luckily, I'd run so far that I was only a few blocks away from my home, anyway.

Rather than use the front entrance, I walked around

the back of the house to the carriage house where George lived. When he answered the door, his graying brows knit together in concern.

"Miss Beckingham? What is wrong?" He leaned out of his door and looked around, as though trying to see if I was being actively attacked.

"Nothing," I said, reaching up to smooth down my hair, which was somehow both sweaty and sticking up in several strange directions. "I'm perfectly fine, but I do require your assistance."

George was more than willing to help me, and I was once again beyond grateful for his loyal service. "I need you to drive to Mr. Wade's home, find Sherborne Sharp standing somewhere along the street, and tell him to meet me at the home of Ivy Holworthy."

I told George I could write the addresses down for him, but he swore he could remember them, and then we both left at the same time.

I could have gone with George, but I wanted a moment alone to speak with Ivy Holworthy. Although she didn't seem to have the same disdain for Sherborne Sharp that her aunt did, I still thought my conversation with her would go more smoothly if I spoke to her alone.

Even though I had some measure of proof that Robert Wade was not being fully honest about his business dealings with Mrs. Holworthy, I still thought the determined woman would be more likely to believe me if she could hear Ivy tell the story in her own words. If Mrs. Holworthy knew that her beloved niece was the one who overheard the strange conversation between Andrew Perring and Robert Wade, she would be more likely to trust my opinion and the letter I'd found. So, I would go to Ivy and ask for her help. Hopefully by the time Sherborne met me there, he wouldn't be too cross.

My feet ached horribly from my impromptu bout of exercise, so I waved down a cab on a main thoroughfare and directed the driver to Ivy's home.

The last time I'd visited Miss Holworthy, it had been a covert affair. Now, I had the driver stop directly in front of her home and climbed out right onto the sidewalk that led to her door. The cab drove away as soon as the driver had his fare, and I mounted the steps, propelled by my recent discovery and my mission to protect Mrs. Holworthy from a man she'd called friend.

Except, when I knocked on the door, there was no answer. I waited several minutes and tried again, but it was the same thing. No one came to the door, and the curtains were pulled closed over the windows.

I sighed in frustration and moved back down the steps.

Clearly, Ivy Holworthy was not home, but what was I to do now? Ordinarily, I would have left and returned later, but Sherborne was to meet me at Ivy's house. If he wasn't angry about me abandoning my post outside of Mr. Wade's home, he would certainly be unhappy if he came to find me at Ivy's, and I was not there.

So, I moved to the left of the stone stairs and waited.

Minutes passed by slowly, dripping away like molasses over a cold table, and my feet still ached. Eventually, I grew tired of even standing and sat down, tucking my legs beneath me on the cool stones.

The street, though near a heavily-populated road, was mostly empty, and I was tucked away out of sight from most of the road, anyway. I would be able to hear and see

Sherborne coming when he did arrive, even if he wouldn't be able to see me.

I had sat there for a long while, considering the speech I would make to try and sway Mrs. Holworthy to distrust her long-time friend, when I heard footsteps approaching. I was about to lean forward to see if it was Sherborne since the steps were hurried, but just before I revealed myself, a blonde man in a dark blue suit mounted the steps and moved onto the porch.

Suddenly nervous, I tucked myself closer to the side of the stairs and the front of the house, wedging myself into the shadows. I knew Ivy wasn't home, so the man would be leaving in another minute, and I hoped he wouldn't see me then. It would be difficult to explain my position, though it was far too late to reveal myself, as well.

There was another round of knocking on the door, but this time, I heard the door open.

"Henry?" I recognized Ivy's voice at once. She spoke in a whisper, her tone astonished. "What are you doing here?"

I wanted to ask Ivy the same question. I'd knocked on her door only a few minutes before, so surely she'd been home.

"I needed to see you," the young man said.

"This is not the way," Ivy whispered back. "A friend of my aunt's was just here a few minutes ago. Do you realize how close you came to being discovered?"

"If I'd come and discovered someone on your porch, I would have kept walking. I wouldn't have risked it," he said. "But you are alone, and I'm desperate to see you."

Ivy sighed, but when she spoke again, her voice was

gentle. "I know I've been busy the past few days. Things with my family have been complicated, and—"

"I know. I should be more sensitive to your loss. I'm sorry."

"It isn't that," Ivy said. "I've never cared about Andrew. His death is only tragic in how it affects his daughters, though I'm beginning to think that even they might be better off without him."

The soft-spoken, kind woman I'd met the day before was nowhere to be found now. This version of Ivy was far more outspoken than the version I'd been familiar with.

"Then why haven't we been able to meet?" Henry asked. "I waited for you in our usual spot, but you didn't come."

Suddenly, I remembered the blonde man Sherborne and I had seen Ivy with the day we'd come to speak with her. This man—Henry—must be one and the same.

I wanted to slip away and give them privacy, if only because it would save me the potential embarrassment of being discovered later and forced to explain my presence, but I couldn't make myself do it. Curiosity kept me rooted to the ground.

"I sent you a message, but you must not have received it," Ivy explained. "I'm going to go and talk to my aunt tonight."

The man whined. It was a pathetic noise, but he seemed to make no secret of how badly he wished to spend time with Ivy. "Again? Can't we have just one evening together? It has been so long."

"Because I've had to be careful," Ivy said sharply. "My aunt can't find out about us before I'm ready. If there is any hope of this plan working, our relationship must remain a secret until I meet with her."

"Our engagement," Henry said lovingly. I could imagine his eyebrows wagging.

Ivy giggled. "It still seems strange to say. I can't believe we will be married."

"The sooner the better," he said.

I heard the distinct sound of kissing and felt my face flame with shame and embarrassment. I should not be hearing this.

"I'm going to go tonight," Ivy said, breaking the kiss. "I've been putting it off because I know I will miss her terribly when she is gone, but...it can't wait any more. I won't put my life on hold for her another minute."

She would miss her? What did that mean? I angled my head up, craning my ear towards the porch as though a closer position would help me better understand what she was saying.

"I've been wanting to do this for so long. I've tried several times, but tonight is the night. It needs to be done."

"Do you want me to come with you?" Henry asked. "I don't want you to do this alone. I can help."

"No. No," Ivy said. "This is my problem, and I have to end it. I don't want you involved. It will be a mess."

A mess?

I didn't think I was breathing. My lungs seemed to have frozen in place, refusing to allow air in or out.

Was Ivy speaking to her secret fiancé about murdering her great aunt?

"Do it tomorrow," Henry said, his voice low and

seductive. "Please. Let me inside, and you can do it first thing tomorrow."

Ivy sighed his name. "She is growing more suspicious every day. I don't want to miss my opportunity to—"

Her words were swallowed in what sounded like a rather forceful kiss. I stayed hidden and still as the two lovers kissed and then, eventually, went inside, closing the door behind them. Even then, I remained in place for a long while before I finally unfolded myself from my hiding place and moved to the sidewalk.

As soon as I did, I heard a loud exhale behind me, and turned to see Sherborne Sharp moving towards me, his features pulled into a deep frown, highlighting the shadows in his face.

"Ten minutes, Alice," he lamented, shaking his head. "I asked you to stay still for ten minutes, and when I came back, you were gone, and the entire Wade household was on high alert. The maids were peeking through the curtains every few minutes. What did you do?"

"I'm sorry, but I saw Mr. Wade leave a few minutes after you left, and I knew he was out of the house. I had to take the opportunity."

"No, you didn't," he said. "What would have happened if you'd been seen?"

I pressed my lips together. "Actually..."

Sherborne dropped his forehead into his hand. "You were seen?"

"I ran straight out of the house and went home. That is why George came to find you and tell you to come here."

"Thank goodness he did, too," Sherborne said sharply. "I didn't know what had happened to you, and the household was behaving so strangely that I thought maybe you were being held prisoner inside. I was moments away from pounding on the door and demanding you be released."

I winced. "I am sorry, but you'll never believe what I've found out."

I wanted to tell Sherborne everything right away, but first, I thought it would be best if we got away from Ivy's home. She was preoccupied for the moment, but if she changed her mind and sent her fiancé away, we could be in trouble.

"Didn't you want to speak with Ivy?" he asked. "Or have you already done that, as well?"

He was bitter that I'd carried on the investigative work without him, and I understood, but I also did not have time to comfort him. There was too much to explain.

"I came to see Ivy because I wanted her to go to Mrs. Holworthy's house with us and try to convince her aunt that Robert Wade could not be trusted."

"You found proof of that?" he asked.

I nodded and reached beneath my blouse to the papers that were still tucked under my waistband. Sherborne turned away sharply when I began bothering with my clothes, pink rising in his usually tanned cheeks. I held the papers out to him, and he took them without looking at me.

"What are these?" He frowned, studying the scribbled numbers.

I explained my theory that Mr. Wade had been mishandling money given to him by Mrs. Holworthy. "However, that isn't the most important piece of evidence I uncovered."

As quickly as possible, I recounted the conversation I'd overheard between Ivy and her fiancé, ignoring Sherborne's snort of amusement when I told him I was hiding beneath the stairs for all of it.

When I finished, he shook his head. "We have to go and see Mrs. Holworthy now."

I agreed. "To inform her that the two most important people in her life have betrayed her."

Our eyes met, and Sherborne gave me a sad smile before extending his arm. It was more than a simple escort. It was an offer of forgiveness. I took it readily.

12

"I think I should go in alone."

Sherborne leaned forward, pressing his forehead to the steering wheel. "Alice. I am here to help you. I *want* to help you. Please let me."

"I know," I said, suddenly remembering the conversation he'd had with my father in the sitting room earlier in the night. "I know you do, and I'm grateful, but if you haven't noticed, Mrs. Holworthy doesn't seem to like you very much."

"Yes, I've caught on to that. However, I think I'll be replaced on the list of people she dislikes most once we tell her what we've discovered tonight."

He had a point. Soon enough, Mrs. Holworthy wouldn't be focusing on her mild dislike of Sherborne. Rather, she'd be horrified to learn that the two people she was closest to in the world had betrayed her.

"I still think she would take the news better if I spoke to her alone," I said. "She is a proud woman, and if there is an audience there for what will likely be her worst moment, she won't respond well."

Sherborne turned and stared at me, eyes assessing. Then, he sighed and nodded his head. "Fine. Yes. I think you are right, but you have to promise me you will be careful."

"I'm always careful," I began to say.

But before I could finish, Sherborne grabbed my hand, clutching it between both of his. "I mean it, Alice. Whatever is going on inside this house, it is complicated and dangerous. If you feel unsafe for even a moment, get out. Don't tell her anything where anyone else will over-hear you. Make sure the conversation is private, and leave as soon as the information is delivered. You were hired to investigate this case, not to defend the woman with your life."

His hand shook around mine, and I could see the sincerity of his concern etched in the lines of his face. Sherborne was frightened for me.

I knew he cared about me. He'd expressed it plenty of times before, but I had never seen his anxieties written so plainly on his features. It was endearing at the same time it was unsettling.

Beyond my family, no one had ever cared for me like this. I didn't know what to do with it.

"I'll be safe," I promised, laying my hand over his. "Wait here, and I'll be back soon."

He clutched my hand for a moment longer and then nodded. Unlike with my promise to him earlier, I knew Sherborne would still be here when I came back. I knew he wouldn't leave me.

N ORA OPENED the door after I knocked. It was the first time I'd seen her since the night of the dinner party. The maid was apparently feeling well enough to come back to work.

"I'm here to see Mrs. Holworthy if she is available?" I said.

"Come in, Miss Beckingham. I'll tell her you are here." It was clear Nora wasn't expecting me, as was only right since I didn't alert anyone to my arrival, but she still showed me to the sitting room and offered me tea. I declined.

The last time I was here, Mrs. Holworthy dismissed me. I didn't know how she would react to the news that I had continued investigating without her consent. I hoped she would forgive me since I had uncovered very suspicious information about her close friend and her niece, but Mrs. Holworthy was a strong-willed woman, and I did not want to pretend to know her mind.

I took a deep breath and folded my hands in my lap, straightening my shoulders. I needed to remain calm, yet firm. I needed her to know the danger she was in, and beyond that, I could do nothing else. Sherborne was right. She hired me to investigate, not to personally protect her. If she chose not to utilize the information I offered, that was her decision.

Would I really walk away, though, if Mrs. Holworthy did not believe me? I wasn't sure I could. Especially since her niece had plans to come to her house the next day and end her life.

I sighed, shoulders slouching under the weight of

responsibility. Mrs. Holworthy chose that moment to appear.

"Miss Beckingham, to what do I owe the pleasure?"

I sat up at once. Mrs. Holworthy was in a deep red velvet dress with a white lace collar and a shawl over her shoulders. The fabric looked heavy and overwhelming on her small frame, but she carried it well and moved to sit in the chair next to the fireplace.

"Is this about your payment?" she continued before I could respond. "I intended to send the money to you through the mail shortly, but if you are eager to collect, I can go and fetch it now."

"No, no," I insisted, shaking my head. "I didn't come here late in the evening and unannounced for money, Mrs. Holworthy."

"Good," she said sharply. "That would have been very rude, and I've come to expect better of you, but it is hard to tell with young people. Some of the manners and ways of life us older generations cling to have been lost on you all. Though, I'm glad to see that is not the case with you. Speaking of less well-mannered people, where is your partner? Mr. Sharp, did he come with you?"

I shook my head. "I came to speak with you alone. It is a rather urgent matter, which is why I came here straight away."

A line formed between her gray brows. "What is it, dear?"

"I know you told me to end the investigation into Andrew's death and the attempts on your life, but I—"

"Went against my wishes," she finished, her mouth puckering into obvious displeasure. "I hired you, Miss Beckingham. That means I have the express power to end your investigation, as well. Continuing on without my permission is an invasion of my privacy and, frankly, damaging to the trust we've built. It is no way to earn a recommendation from me."

"I'm sorry," I said earnestly, cutting her off before she could continue. "Truly, I'm sorry you feel that way, and from this point on, I will do as you ask in regards to the case, but I discovered information that is pertinent to you."

"I will not pay you for it, so you may as well keep it to yourself," she said, lifting her chin in defiance.

"Mrs. Holworthy," I pleaded. "The information concerns your safety, and I promise you will want to know it."

"And I promise you I won't!" Anger flared in her eyes and the dark red color of her dress seemed to be leeching out of the fabric and into her neck. Her hand shook on the armrest of the chair for a second before she tucked her fingers into a side pocket and pulled out the small metal tin of pills. She retrieved a flat pill, placed it on her tongue, and sucked on it as it dissolved in her mouth.

If the woman had some kind of heart condition, I didn't want to aggravate it. I didn't want to make her ill, but making her ill would be better than losing her life entirely as her niece planned for her tomorrow, wouldn't it?

"Ivy wishes to kill you," I said plainly, not giving her the chance to ignore me. "She has a secret fiancé, and I overheard them talking of their plans to come here tomorrow and—"

Mrs. Holworthy frowned, one brow arched. "You heard Ivy say she would kill me?"

I replayed the conversation in my head and shrugged. "She didn't say the words exactly, but she said that she'd been trying to do something for awhile, but hadn't managed to yet. Tomorrow would be the day she'd finally take care of it, and until then, she wanted her relationship with her fiancé to remain a secret."

Saying the words out loud, it did sound like rather thin evidence, but I still believed it shed enough doubt on Ivy's trustworthiness to concern Mrs. Holworthy.

"Perhaps, she intends to come here tomorrow and tell me of her fiancé's existence?"

"She said she would miss you," I argued.

"Because I will surely disown her once she tells me," Mrs. Holworthy said. "She wants to tell me the truth about her romance before I discover it elsewhere. I'm sure that is what she meant."

"But how can you be certain?"

Mrs. Holworthy stood up and waved her hand, gesturing for me to follow her towards the door, but I stayed seated, openly disregarding the woman's wishes until she could provide an adequate answer to my question.

"Because I know the people close to me," she said. "You are a detective, so surely you understand when a person has a natural ability to read others. I have that, as well. I know upon first meeting whether a person is trustworthy or not. I am able to tell whether they are selfish or generous, astute or obtuse. When it comes to my own family, that ability is magnified tenfold. I know Ivy Holworthy as though she were my own daughter, and I do not believe for a second this information you have brought me. You were released from my employ earlier today, and you have grown desperate. Perhaps, it is money troubles. Though you do not know me, I know of you, Alice Beckingham. I know the troubles your family has endured, and I know you misjudged your own brother. You likely did not think him a murderer, did you?"

I gasped, shocked by the acid in Mrs. Holworthy's tone. I understood she was probably offended by my words against her niece, but still, I never expected her to go so harshly after my family.

"I do not care about your money," I insisted. "Feel free not to pay me at all. It would serve me right for continuing the investigation beyond your wishes. The simple truth is that I felt something wrong in this situation, and I couldn't walk away until I knew I'd uncovered it. You believe Andrew attempted to kill you and instead killed himself, but I know that is not what occurred. I have reason to believe Robert Wade executed the murder of Andrew Perring due to money he has stolen from you. I have a letter Andrew wrote to Robert and a ledger that shows discrepancies in the money you provided him and the money he invested in—"

"Enough!" Mrs. Holworthy slashed a hand through the air, the velvet garments around her body swaying with the movement. Something clattered out of her pocket and white spots spilled across the floor. They were her pills.

Immediately, I knelt down to begin scooping them up, but Mrs. Holworthy snorted in frustration. "Leave them. The maid can help me. I want you out of my house. You have come here and accused the people closest to me of crimes I know they couldn't have committed and—"

"You believed someone close to you wanted you dead. You hired me for that very purpose, yet now you reject the information I've found." I'd wanted to remain emotionless throughout this discussion, but Mrs. Holworthy was no longer being rational. She had cruelly attacked my family and my abilities, and was now neglecting to give any credence to the information I'd uncovered. It didn't make sense that she had hired me for this task, yet now refused to believe me.

I gathered a handful of the circular, flat white pills. Each pill was identical. Whatever their purpose, Mrs. Holworthy liked to keep a great many of them very close to her should she need them.

"Because I know your theory to be impossible," the woman shouted. "Andrew sought to kill me with some kind of poison, and he poisoned himself by mistake. The drunkard regularly drank from every half-remaining glass on the table after meals, so I'm not surprised. He wanted me dead, and now he is gone. I have no regret and would happily move on from the matter if you would leave me be and allow it."

Suddenly, the memory of Andrew helping clear the table came back to me. When Nora had come to take away our dinner dishes, Andrew had gone to his mother-in-law's place setting and retrieved her wine glass. He'd carried it into the kitchen where, minutes later, he died in the back corner of the pantry...an empty wine glass sitting on the shelf above his head.

I froze, knelt on the floor, my hands clutching a handful of identical pills. Pills that were white and flat. Pills that Mrs. Holworthy laid on her tongue to dissolve.

A cold dread slipped down my spine, leaving goose-bumps in its wake.

"Do I need to sort these pills in any way?" I asked, trying to keep my voice level. "Are they all the same or do you have more than one medication. I'd hate to mix them up for you."

Mrs. Holworthy sighed in frustration. "I only have the one medication. They are all the same."

Her pills were all supposed to be the same, yet, the night of the dinner party her pill had been misshapen. It had been an oblong pill that I recalled her washing down with a long drink of wine. Wine she immediately determined tasted too bitter and refused to take another drink of. She also barred her son-in-law from getting a refill of his own glass when he requested one from the server.

"Are you certain?" I asked.

"Am I certain that I only have one medication?" she asked with a sneer. "Yes, Miss Detective, I am positive that the pills I've been taking daily for the previous decade are the only medication I need."

I poured the handful of pills I'd gathered into the metal tin, closed the box, and stood to hand it to her, my fingers shaking slightly with adrenaline as I said: "Then, if not a medication, what was the purpose of the pill you put in your mouth the night of your dinner party?"

Mrs. Holworthy made as if to respond, but then her mouth fell open, and her eyes went wide with shock. It was only a momentary loss of composure, but it was enough to tell me that I'd been wrong about everything from the start.

"I've noticed you place these circular pills on your

tongue to dissolve," I said, mimicking the action myself. "However, the night of the party, you placed an oblong pill into your cheek and then followed it with a drink of wine."

The color that had earlier been gathering in the old woman's neck and cheeks drained out, only a grayish white left in its stead.

"I didn't find the wine bitter at all, but you did. You took a long drink of it and then determined it was no longer palatable."

She pressed her lips together, wrinkles radiating out from the puckered expression. Her eyes wouldn't meet mine. "What are you on about, Miss Beckingham? Now that you've accused my friend and my niece of crimes, are you here to do the same to me? Is it a crime to not finish a glass of wine?"

"No, of course not," I said with a humorless laugh. "Though, it is a crime to spit a poisoned pill into a glass with the knowledge that someone else will drink it. I do believe murder is a crime often punishable by death."

She met my eyes for the first time in several minutes, and I watched the shift of emotions. I observed panic alter to anger and then, finally, to an amused resignation. Her lip curled into a malicious smile. She was an old woman, but a chill still worked through me.

"There is no evidence of the crime," she said, voice low and serious. "Poor Andrew consumed it all. There is nothing left for anyone to find, and I will not be charged with anything."

Even though I knew Mrs. Holworthy was guilty, hearing her admit it so boldly still shocked me. I shook my head. "Why would you do that? His children are your grandchildren. Do you not care that their only living parent is now dead?"

"If you can call him a parent," she snapped. "If Andrew cared for his girls at all, he showed it by arriving home too drunk to speak with them. By spending the money meant for their upbringing on women and cards and drink. Is that the parent I was supposed to entrust the last of my blood family to?"

I wanted to sit down on the sofa behind me—my legs felt unsteady—but I didn't want to lower my guard. I didn't expect Mrs. Holworthy to lunge across the room at me, but I also couldn't discount her. Not now that I knew what she was capable of.

"Andrew refused to leave the girls in my care, and he regularly threatened that he would leave and take them with him where I'd never see them again. Can you imagine something so cruel?"

"I can, actually," I admitted. "Murder seems to me a rather cruel action."

She rolled her eyes. "You are young yet, Miss Beckingham. You don't understand what it means to protect those you love. Life is not so clearly defined as you'd like to believe."

I thought of Edward and his death. He had murdered a man in an effort to protect our sister. Then, he had been murdered himself. Some would call that justice, but I wouldn't.

I knew my brother was not a good man. I knew he had made mistakes, but I also knew the lives of those he left behind were worse without him. Every person, whether they were aware of it or not, had a web that extended beyond them, touching other people and other lives. Andrew Perring, despite his faults and vices, had three girls who loved him very much. They would not appreciate what their grandmother had done in their names.

"Perhaps you are right." I shrugged, not believing that possible at all. "Though, I'll suggest you save your breath in favor of convincing the police of that theory."

Mrs. Holworthy narrowed her eyes for a moment and then let out a bitter laugh. "As I've said, the evidence is gone, Miss Beckingham. Andrew drank it. Very observant of you, by the way, to notice the difference in my pills. I coated a cyanide capsule in a thin shell that would protect me while it was in my mouth momentarily, but would begin to dissolve as soon as it touched the wine. As the glass sat in front of me, the pill dissolved, and by the time Andrew greedily drank it down in the back of the kitchen, he had no idea it was laced with anything at all. He died in mere minutes."

I'd seen it happen. I'd watched Mrs. Holworthy spit the pill back into the glass. I'd seen Andrew pick it up. Still, I hadn't been able to put the pieces together because I thought I was there to protect Mrs. Holworthy.

"So, your employing me was nothing more than a distraction?" I asked.

"A diversion," she said. "If suspicion did turn to me, I would be able to show the authorities that I'd been concerned about my own life. You were nothing more than a prop in my play. Why else would I hire you, a wholly inexperienced detective, rather than one of the many professionals I could afford?"

My pride bruised from the blow, but there was solace in knowing I'd uncovered her plot, regardless.

"I can't be so inexperienced if I found you out," I said. "Or is my discovery more a remark on the faultiness of your plan?"

"You've surprised me," she admitted. "I didn't expect you to uncover my plot, but now that you have, you have a choice."

"Do I?"

She nodded and took a step towards me, head tipped to the side, eyes thoughtful. "You can walk away and forget this happened. I'll pay you handsomely for it, believe me."

I backed away, refusing to put myself any closer to the murderess. "And what is my second option?"

Mrs. Holworthy's mouth twisted to the side in disappointment, and she shrugged as though regretting there wasn't another way. "Or, you die."

Fear gripped my chest, but I pushed it down and shook my head. "I won't be dying here today."

I could fight Mrs. Holworthy if it came to it, but it shouldn't. Sherborne was sitting outside in his car. All I had to do was run into the hallway, make it to the door, and get outside. Then, we could go directly to the police. Mrs. Holworthy wouldn't be able to catch me.

"Let that be another point on which we disagree," she said, her face stretching into a cold smile.

I knew any further conversation between us would be a waste of time. She wished me dead, and I wished to leave. Desperately.

So, I spun around and ran for the doorway.

Just as I got into the hall, I saw a tall figure before me, sheathed in shadows, and I nearly sighed in relief.

Sherborne had come inside to check on me. He'd

heard what Mrs. Holworthy was guilty of and we would escape together.

However, when the figure turned, I saw the round face that looked nothing like the long, square jaw of my friend. I saw the gray hair and sunken eyes and thick mustache.

I saw Robert Wade.

"Miss Beckingham?" he said, face pinched in concern. "Where's the fire? Hopefully there has not been another."

He was not exactly the friendly face I'd hoped to find, but he was innocent of the murder of Andrew Perring, after all, and deserved to know what his friend had done.

"We must leave," I said, skidding to a stop before I smacked directly into his chest. "Mrs. Holworthy killed Andrew Perring, and we must go now."

Confusion flickered in his eyes before they narrowed seriously. "You know this for a fact?"

"She does," Mrs. Holworthy said from behind me. "The little detective uncovered our plan."

I tried to push past Robert Wade to get to the door, but he threw out an arm to block me. That was when I recognized what Mrs. Holworthy had said.

Our plan.

I looked up at Robert, and he was staring down at me, eyes dark and fathomless. Fear snaked around my neck, blocking the air from reaching my lungs.

He grabbed my arm and lifted me so violently my feet nearly left the ground. "I suppose you won't be leaving then, after all."

13

I struggled against his hold, but though the man was along in years, he had not lost his strength. His hand was an immovable cuff around my wrist, and I could not pull myself free.

"Please," I begged, my voice rising so anyone else in the house would hear. "Please. Help!"

Sherborne was just outside. Just beyond the front door. If only I could scream loudly enough or get to a window.

"There is no use shouting," Mrs. Holworthy said, following my struggling progress down the hallway. "I sent Nora home just after you arrived, and the girls and their nanny are in the country house for the week. The children needed time away from the mourning happening here. We are all alone."

Alone.

I cursed myself for not taking Sherborne up on his offer to accompany me inside. Why had I insisted on going alone? Why did I always insist on going alone? If he had been with me, I wouldn't be in this predicament.

Robert Wade grabbed me with both hands around my middle, lifting my feet off the floor, and carried me into Mrs. Holworthy's private sitting room. The very room where she'd been when the fire had supposedly started outside the door.

I now suspected she'd started that herself, as well, as another diversion from her true plan.

The woman had been plotting her son-in-law's death for some time, which only confirmed how deeply in trouble I was now. She would not be so quick to let me ruin her plan. What was the death of one young detective in the name of protecting her grandchildren?

I had to fight and escape or I would surely die.

Robert threw me forward into a chair. I landed on the arm of it, and immediately felt the press of something cold and hard into my side.

The pistol.

It was still concealed beneath my clothes from when I'd broken into Robert Wade's house. If I could grab it, I could force the deadly duo to either release me or be shot.

However, before I could draw the weapon, Robert grabbed my right arm and yanked it behind my back, hauling me to my feet. Then, he did the same with my left, gathering them both together in his large hands, making it impossible for me to reach anything.

"You've been busy tonight," he said, his voice a hot whisper in my ear. "I received word that an intruder had come into my home. Strange, though, as it was a young woman. Short brown hair, a heart-shaped face. Do you know anyone of that description?"

Mrs. Holworthy's face was smug and amused. She claimed she'd killed Andrew out of necessity, but I suspected she'd found more enjoyment in it than she would let herself admit.

"I discovered you were stealing money from Mrs. Holworthy," I spat. Perhaps, if I could turn the two killers on one another, they'd forget about me long enough so I could grab the weapon. It was not an ideal plan, but it was the only one I had. "A letter from Andrew Perring proved that he knew of your misdeeds, and I found ledgers, as well. You kept it all in an unlocked case. Not very wise."

"I intended to burn it," he growled. "The police looked through my files the other day, and I removed those to keep my name cleared. I planned to dispose of them."

"You knew of his deception?" I asked, looking over my shoulder at Mrs. Holworthy.

"How else do you think I convinced him to help me with my problem," she said, referring to her deceased son-in-law as though he were a slight inconvenience. "He had to repay me in some way."

"And I was glad to do it," Robert Wade said, his hands loosening ever so slightly around my wrists. "If the poison had not worked, I would have feigned an argument with the man and killed him in my own self-defense. Everyone at the party saw how drunk he was. It wouldn't have been difficult to believe he'd attack me."

"That is why you went into the kitchen after him," I

said. "To distract the maid from his death, but also to cause a scene should he not take your poisoned bait."

Robert didn't respond, but I knew I was right. Regardless of what happened that evening, Andrew Perring would have died.

"And you would work with a man you cannot trust, Mrs. Holworthy? What makes you believe he won't turn on you?"

Mrs. Holworthy smiled. "Because if I die in any uncertain circumstances, Mr. Wade gets nothing. The only way he can stand to inherit any of my wealth is if he remains loyal to me."

At one point, I'd admired the relationship between Mrs. Holworthy and Mr. Wade. They were a man and a woman who had been friendly companions for years. At times, I even wondered if Sherborne and I could work together in the same way.

Now, however, I could see their relationship for what it was: manipulation and deceit and greed.

"You two aren't even friends," I realized with a start. "You use one another. You are cruel and manipulative. How you haven't killed one another already is beyond me."

Mrs. Holworthy sighed. "If there is anything you should have learned from me by now, Miss Beckingham, it is that I do everything alone. I do not depend on the generosity or kindness of others. Rather, I take what I need and do what I must to get what I want. Mr. Wade has made himself useful to me many times over the years. When my husband fell into grief after the loss of our son in the war and began letting our business and social connections slide, Mr. Wade helped me to gain control of the estate."

Gain control of the estate... I gasped. "You killed your own husband?"

"It was a mercy killing," she said with a roll of her eyes at my dramatics. "He was a miserable man lost to grief."

"My name was written into the will for that scheme," Robert said behind me, his voice filled with pride at his accomplishment.

"And...your daughter?" I asked hesitantly.

Mrs. Holworthy's eyes sharpened, her mouth pressing into a thin white line. "Don't suggest it. I would have rather died myself than lost my daughter. However, after her passing, I promised myself I would do whatever was necessary to protect her daughters. So I have, and so I will continue to do. Regardless of what action that promise requires of me."

I shook my head, unable to grasp the tangle of horrors I'd found myself ensnared in. I'd taken Mrs. Holworthy at face value. She asked me to investigate anyone who might want to harm her, and I never for a moment considered that she could be the one capable of murder. In the end, I'd recognized it, but not soon enough to save myself.

"What will you do to me?" I asked. "How will you explain it?"

Mrs. Holworthy began to pace across the small space, eyes narrowed in thought. "You've made it quite easy for me, Alice. Just tonight you broke into Mr. Wade's home and were seen by his housemaid. She will be able to identify your body for the police later and confirm the story.

"Then, all that will remain to explain is that you came here next. You broke in, overeager after having been hired as a detective for the first time, and were killed by a single blow to the head when Mr. Wade encountered you surprisingly in the sitting room."

I cursed myself for being so reckless. For giving Mrs. Holworthy everything she needed to cover up my murder as nothing more than a tragic accident. However, there was still something she did not know: Sherborne Sharp sat waiting outside.

He would be expecting me to come out to the car soon, and when I didn't, he'd come and check on me. I knew it. I simply had to stay alive until then.

"Nora answered the door for me," I said. "She'll know you're lying."

"You visited with me, it's true," Mrs. Holworthy said. "But I told you to end your investigation, and you were very upset. You left in anger, and then returned later without my permission or knowledge. That is when Mr. Wade, not wanting to spend the evening in his own home since it had just been ransacked, came over for a drink and found an intruder."

The ease with which she concocted the lie stunned me into silence.

"Unless you see any other faults with my plan, I think we will get it over with now," she said. "It is getting late, and I do not want to deal with the police early into the morning the way I was forced to with Andrew."

Yes, better get on with it. I'd hate for my death to be an inconvenience to her rest.

Sherborne was outside, and I could mention that to the two of them, but if I did, I worried about what would happen to Sherborne. They could keep me tied inside and then go out to his car and spin some lie to get him to come in. Then, they could do away with him, as well. Mrs. Holworthy was a professional when it came to deception, and I had no doubts she could concoct a story that would account for Sherborne's death, as well.

No, if I stayed quiet on Sherborne being outside, he would survive and be able to tell the truth. He was as good a detective as I was, and if I couldn't escape this plot, he wouldn't stop until he solved the case of how I died. He would bring justice to my family, and that was some kind of solace.

Mrs. Holworthy nodded, and at her silent command, Robert Wade gripped both of my hands with one of his and reached for a large statue on the end table between the chair and sofa. It was carved in the likeness of a horse with a long snout and tail, but it was the base that concerned me. The horse stood upon a large stone block with sharp edges. Corners that would break through my scalp with ease. Certainly, one blow was all it would take.

I yelped and began to thrash, my legs kicking out at whatever they could find.

Robert Wade tightened his hold on my hands, pausing his grab for the statue in an attempt to regain control over me.

"Hold still," he growled, as if I would listen to him. If I did, it would be the last thing I ever did.

I arched my back and hurled my weight forward, forcing the man to stumble. Mrs. Holworthy barked orders at him from the side of the room, but I ignored her. I was singularly focused on freeing my arms, grabbing my pistol, and getting out of this room.

Robert widened his stance, trying to gain more traction, but in my thrashing, my foot tripped over his. My weight went suddenly forward, and Robert fell with me.

My face and chest slammed into the floor, and I saw stars in my vision, but there was no time to recover. No time to stop.

His hand had slipped from around my wrists in the fall, and I was able to free my arms.

I shifted my weight to my left side so I could reach into the waistband at my right hip and grab the pistol, but just as I got my hand beneath my shirt, Robert's weight fell over my back, crushing me down into the floor.

His hands fumbled down my arms, trying to pull them back behind my back, but I used all of my remaining strength to keep my arm pinned in front of me. My fingers brushed against the cool metal of the pistol. All I needed was enough space between my body and the floor to pull it free. Just a centimeter. A fraction of that, even.

The man's breath was hot and stale on the back of my neck. He was wheezing, clearly exhausted from our fight already, and for one second, I let my body relax. I eased into the floor, loosening my muscles, allowing him to believe that I was spent. That he'd overpowered me.

I felt the second he thought he'd won. He shifted his weight to the hand he had pressed into the floor, and in that brief moment, I pulled the pistol from my hip, raised it towards the ceiling, and fired off a shot.

The sound was powerful and sharp. I knew to expect it, and it still made me jump with surprise.

Mrs. Holworthy screamed and, operating entirely on

instinct, Robert Wade rolled away from me and raised his arms over his head.

I crawled to my feet, my chest heaving with adrenaline and exhaustion, and held the pistol in front of me. "Don't move."

Mrs. Holworthy stared at me in abject horror, and then her gaze flickered down to the still trembling man on the floor in front of me. Disgust curled her lip, and she shook her head. When her eyes returned to me, they were wide and deceptively earnest.

"I can give you more money than you can imagine," she said. "I can fund your life for the rest of your days. Shoot him, and I will tell everyone it was in self-defense. We will tell everyone he killed Andrew, and when confronted, he became violent. You have his motive—the letter and the ledgers. You will gain the glory for solving this case and enough money to never work again if you should please."

"No amount of money would ever convince me to allow you to get away with your crimes. I will not be tempted by money to sell my very soul."

I leveled the weapon at Mrs. Holworthy and kept one eye on where Robert Wade was sitting on the floor as I moved towards the door.

When I reached it, I grabbed the handle behind me and turned the knob slowly. But just as the latch released, the door burst open, and there was a manly yell behind me.

I shouted and spun around, gun swinging wildly, but before I could aim it at the new threat, I realized it was Sherborne Sharp standing behind me.

His eyes were wide, face pale, and he studied me,

assessing me for any sign of damage or injury. "Alice? Alice, are you hurt? I heard a shot and—"

The sound of pounding footsteps behind me caught my attention, but before I could do anything, Sherborne shoved me aside, stepped into the doorway, and threw a quick, effective punch at the figure of Robert Wade rushing towards the door.

Mr. Wade crumpled to the floor immediately, blood flowing from his nose.

Sherborne shook out his hand, and then wrapped a protective arm around my waist. "Keep your weapon on him."

I lifted the gun and held it steadily on Mr. Wade, though Sherborne's punch seemed to have knocked him unconscious.

"They both killed Andrew, and they intended to kill me, as well," I said.

"Who was shot?"

"No one, I think," I said, looking at Mr. Wade and then Mrs. Holworthy, who was watching the proceedings with a vulture-like gaze. I couldn't believe I had never noticed it before, the way she studied people, waiting to strike at any weakness. I'd seen it as a strength before. As a kind of resilience in the face of a world that wanted her to be quiet and demure. Now, however, I realized it was all manipulation. She projected confidence and outspokenness, making everyone believe she hadn't the ability to keep a secret. When really, her life was built upon them. Her personality was yet another distraction, and I'd fallen for it.

"I was growing worried waiting for you, and then I heard the gunshot and—" Sherborne shivered. "I thought

I would come in here to find you dead, Alice. I thought you were gone and—"

"I fired the shot," I said, interrupting him. "Mr. Wade tried to kill me, but I managed to startle him with a warning shot. I was on my way outside when you arrived."

Sherborne opened his mouth to say something and then shook his head, thinking better of it. "We need to alert the police. Help me tie Mr. Wade's hands and feet, and then I will remain here while you call for help."

After a day of making plans and crisscrossing all over town, I was grateful for Sherborne's decisiveness. I kept my weapon trained on Mrs. Holworthy while Sherborne went to a closet down the hall and found a blanket. He tore the blanket into strips and then bound the material around the still unconscious man's hands and feet. Then, he moved towards Mrs. Holworthy.

"Are you so frightened of an elderly woman?" she asked.

"Not ordinarily," he said. "However, I am afraid of being in the same room as a monster."

The outspoken woman suddenly had nothing to say, and she did not fight as Sherborne tied her hands together tightly.

Before I left the room, I pressed my gun into his hand. "I'll be back in a few moments."

His eyes moved over my face slowly, and it still felt as though he was assessing me, trying to convince himself I was fine. I wanted to ease his mind, but it would have to wait.

～

THE POLICE ARRIVED within fifteen minutes, and just as Mrs. Holworthy feared would happen, we were all interviewed through the rest of the evening and into the early hours of the morning. Though, she hadn't expected to find herself as the suspect.

Mr. Robert Wade was loaded into a vehicle and transported to the hospital to be seen by a doctor, but we received word within the hour that he'd awoken and, under the slightest bit of pressure, confessed to everything. Despite her skillful deceptions, Mrs. Holworthy's story began to unravel after that.

As it turned out, she'd been able to so fully fool the police that they'd done very little investigating into her as a suspect. But within a few minutes of searching through her personal files, they found suspicious correspondences between herself and Robert Wade, along with a small package of cyanide capsules and handwritten instructions for how to safely coat them to temporarily protect a person from their effects.

Sherborne and I sat in the sitting room as the officers moved from room to room, one of them occasionally coming in to ask a question about the evening's events or to have me retell what I witnessed the evening of the dinner party. The longer we sat, the more exhausted I became until I laid my head on Sherborne's shoulder, desperate to close my eyes and go to sleep.

The clock in the hallway chimed one in the morning when an officer with dark circles beneath his eyes came in. "I think that is all we need from the two of you this evening. Do you require an escort to your residence?"

"I can handle it," Sherborne said, standing and

extending a hand to help me, as well. "Thank you, officer."

"Thank you," I repeated blearily.

Before we could reach the door, the officer cleared his throat. "One more thing, Miss Beckingham. There was a report of a break-in at Mr. Wade's home earlier this evening. Would you happen to know anything about that?"

"Mr. Wade may have mentioned that prior to being knocked unconscious," I said coyly.

"We would hate to waste our time looking for the culprit if there is no chance of a similar break-in occurring in the future."

I bit my lip. "I imagine the culprit only acted out of a sense of urgency. I'm sure there won't be any repeat offences."

The officer's mouth curled into a reluctant smile. "That is welcome news, and I hope you are correct. Perhaps, the person who broke in should leave these kinds of matters to the professionals."

"Perhaps, they should," I said, deciding now was not the time to remind the officer that had it not been for *that person*, two murderers would still be walking free.

Sherborne helped me shrug into my coat and then wrapped his arm around mine, leading me gently down the stairs and to his car. When we got inside, the vehicle was dark and cool, and moonlight slanted through the windshield, giving Sherborne a ghostly glow. He turned to me, and his eyes were dark as the sky above.

"I should have gone inside with you."

There was a deep sadness in his voice, guilt and regret twisting into a tight knot of pain. All evening, he'd been stoic and professional, speaking evenly with the police and listening as I told my story. But not anymore.

Instinctively, I reached across the seat and grabbed his hand. "Sherborne, no. Don't do that. I told you not to come."

"I shouldn't have listened," he said. "Watching you walk into that house alone felt wrong to me, but I stayed here. I sat in this very spot while you were nearly killed inside. If Robert Wade had been allowed to carry through with his plan...if you'd died in there while I did nothing, I never would have forgiven myself."

"I didn't die, though." I curled my fingers more tightly around his, grateful for the warmth that poured from him. "I am safe and well, and the two murderers have been apprehended. Everything is all right."

Sherborne's brow was still furrowed in frustration, and I knew he hadn't yet forgiven himself, so I continued, voice low.

"You value my opinion, Sherborne. It is more important to me that you trust me than it is that you weren't there the moment I found myself in trouble," I said. "As soon as you became aware something was wrong, you ran headlong into danger, having no idea what to expect. You could have been killed yourself, but you came inside to find me. Do you not realize how incredibly brave that is?"

"It isn't so brave."

"It is," I insisted.

He shook his head. "I didn't run in there to save you, Alice. I ran in there to save myself. Losing you in any way, but especially like that, would have destroyed me. You must know that."

Suddenly, the words inside of me were gone. I could

think of nothing suitable to say. I couldn't think of a single word worthy of the ones Sherborne had just given me. So, instead, I squeezed his hand and let my thumb run across his rough knuckles.

He brought our joined hands to his lips, pressed a kiss to my suddenly flushed skin, and then started his car and took me home.

14

"How could there already be a story in the paper?" I asked, staring down at the article on the front page. It wasn't above the fold, but the headline would be enough to catch attention: *Widow Arrested for Multiple Murders of Own Family.*

"How could you possibly have failed to tell us a thing about it?" Mama asked with the same stern expression she'd worn earlier when she'd woken me suddenly from bed.

"No one was awake when I came home," I argued for what felt like the hundredth time. "I planned to tell you first thing this morning."

Mama snorted, and Papa reached across the breakfast table and plucked the paper from my hand. "You ran out of this house with the assistance of your sister, who is apparently a very talented actress." He leveled a scathing look at Catherine, but she pretended to be too busy patting Hazel's back to notice. "And then you and that young man nearly got yourselves killed."

"Sherborne didn't do a thing wrong," I said. "He risked his life to save mine after I put myself in danger."

"You shouldn't have been there in the first place," he mumbled.

"Lucky I was, considering the killer would otherwise have gotten away with the crime."

Papa muttered something under his breath, but I could tell that even he didn't have an argument for that. My investigation had been more thorough than the police investigation, and I'd caught a murderer. Two murderers, in fact. Even if no one else was going to compliment my accomplishment, I would be proud of myself.

"Where is Mr. Sharp?" Catherine asked. "Will we be seeing him today?"

"If he is wise, then no," Papa said.

"James," Mama whispered, nudging him under the table.

"He and I will be going to see Mrs. Holworthy's niece this morning," I said, ignoring both of my parents. "I'd like to speak with her and explain what I found and what happened. In fact, I should be going soon. He and I are to meet at her house."

"Oh, but you'll miss Charles arriving," Catherine said. "He finalized the sale of the Yorkshire property and is set to arrive late this morning."

"Yes, don't you think it is time to be done with the Holworthy family?" Mama asked. "You've had your fun, and now it is time to focus on other tasks."

"Fun?" Papa shouted, nearly spilling his tea. "Is being attacked by murderers a new hobby? If so, I forbid Alice from ever having fun again."

Mama sighed. "That isn't what I meant, James."

"Your mother is right, though," he continued. "You are not to take on any more cases. It is not safe."

"You did not forbid Rose from becoming a detective!"

"Because Rose is not my daughter," Papa responded flatly, as though the matter was settled.

"And if she had been, you would have stopped her?"

"Rose has been through many trials in her life, Alice. You know that. She was forced to grow a tough skin. You, my daughter, do not need to do that."

I considered a calm, measured response to his answer, but before I could stop myself, I pushed away from the table with alarming force and stood up. My chest heaved with frustration and words that had been gathering inside of me for longer than even I had realized.

Every eye turned to me, and I realized all at once that I needed to speak up for myself. Sherborne had come to my defense twice now where my family was concerned, but it was time I voiced my own desires. It was time I informed my family how things would be moving forward, regardless of whether they appreciated it or not.

"Have I not also struggled?" I asked plainly. "My eldest brother murdered a man, went to prison, and was killed. Is that not the kind of experience that makes one stronger?"

"Alice," Papa said, averting his eyes. "We are not going to talk about—"

"About the missing member of our family?" I pressed. "For so long, I thought that was the answer. Perhaps, if I stayed quiet on the subject of Edward, my parents would heal and be happy again. Maybe if I didn't think about him, I could carry on with life as usual. I thought if I didn't touch the pain, then it would go away, but it never did. So, I decided to do something about it."

Mama frowned. "What do you mean?"

"I wasn't going to tell you this," I said. "I thought it would only bring more pain for you all, but now I think carrying it by myself was a mistake."

"Alice, are you sure?" Catherine said softly.

I nodded to her, and our parents glanced back and forth between the two of us, obviously confused.

"I demand to know what is going on in my own house," my father said, pressing a finger into the top of the table. "Right now."

Slowly and carefully, I began to relay to them the story of their son's crimes and death. I explained that Edward had contacted a powerful criminal to procure the poison he used to kill his victim, Mr. Matcham, and I explained how that criminal sought Edward out once he was imprisoned.

"Edward died because of his own mistakes, yes," I admitted. "But he would still be alive if the police had captured The Chess Master sooner."

My parents were stunned by the revelation. We all knew Edward had been murdered, but to know it was more than just a random death, but rather a planned killing, was a lot to take in.

My mother shook her head. "Has this Chess Master been caught yet?"

I nodded. "I found him while I was in New York, and now he is dead."

Their eyes all widened. Even Catherine's. That was part of the story I had not told anyone yet.

"I began these investigations because I wanted to

understand what happened to my brother," I explained. "Everything I've done over this past year was in search of the truth about Edward, but while uncovering that truth, I uncovered one about myself, as well. I like detective work. I enjoy finding the pieces of a puzzle and putting them together. I enjoy bringing people a measure of peace in hard circumstances. I enjoy fighting for truth and justice."

"Those are all admirable things, Alice," Mama said. "But your safety is what is important to us and—"

"And I appreciate your concern, but it will not sway my resolve." I set my jaw and faced them all, hoping I looked as resolute as I felt. "I will do my best to be safe, but from this point on, my future is in my hands. I will determine my path, and I hope you will support me."

Catherine's mouth pulled into a small smile that she tried her best to hide, but both of my parents still looked concerned, brows drawn inward.

"For now, however, I need to meet my partner and speak with Ivy Holworthy."

I nodded my head in a farewell, turned on my heel, and left the house at once, going so quickly I left my coat hanging in the hall.

~

"WHERE ON EARTH IS YOUR COAT?" Sherborne asked when we met on the sidewalk outside of Ivy Holworthy's home. "You are going to freeze."

He began shrugging out of his own jacket, but I waved him away. "We will be inside in a moment. I'll be fine until then. My coat is at home where I left it after making a rather dramatic exit. Going back to get it would have ruined the effect."

"A dramatic exit?" he asked, dark eyebrow raised. "More dramatic than your sister screaming at the bottom of the stairs?"

"Perhaps, not that dramatic," I admitted with a small laugh.

"Will I hear this story at some point?"

I nodded towards Ivy's front door. "After."

Unlike the last several times I'd called on Ivy Holworthy, I sent word ahead of our arrival. Life had been unexpected enough for her. I didn't think I should add unexpected visitors to that list, as well.

As it was, she opened the door before I could even knock. Her eyes were red-rimmed and swollen from crying.

"Oh, Ivy," I said softly. I didn't know the young woman, but I had the urge to pull her into a hug. Before I could, a blonde-haired man appeared behind her and laid a hand on her shoulder.

"Sit down, dear. I told you I'd get the door," he said gently.

"The girls?" Ivy asked, her voice hoarse. "Where are they?"

"Let's talk inside." I suggested it because Ivy looked close to collapsing, though the fact that I was shivering had a small amount to do with it, as well.

Ivy led us into her finely decorated sitting room. The space was small, but homey, and the man I knew as her fiancé tucked a quilt around Ivy's legs after she sat and silently offered her a cup of tea. She took it with a weepy smile, wrapping her hands around the warmth.

Neither of them offered me or Sherborne anything, which didn't offend me in the slightest. Ivy was far too worried about her family, and her fiancé was overflowing with worry over Ivy.

"Do you know where the girls are?" Ivy asked. "I haven't been able to get any word from anyone. The police are keeping tight lipped about everything until they know the full scope of who was involved in this plot, as if I ever could have been involved in murdering someone."

Ivy nearly choked on the idea, so I decided not to inform her that I'd gone to Mrs. Holworthy's house last night under the suspicion that Ivy was the sole killer.

"The girls are at the country estate. Or, at least, that is what your aunt told me before...everything happened."

Ivy sighed. "That is what I hoped. I didn't want to think of them being pulled from their beds and taken who knows where in the middle of the night."

Her lower lip began to tremble at just the thought, and her fiancé wrapped his arm around her shoulders. I smiled at his kindness, and he returned the expression. "I'm John Housh, by the way. Ivy's fiancé."

Ivy turned to him suddenly, eyes wide in surprise. "No one knows that yet."

"Actually, I did," I admitted before the two of them could discuss it any further. "I hope you'll forgive the intrusion, but I've done some rather thorough investigating."

Ivy shook her head and let her shoulders slouch forward. "I suppose there is no need for it to be a secret now. We were only keeping it quiet until I could find the courage to tell my aunt. I wanted to please her so badly, and to think, all this time, she'd been..."

She began to tremble again. John pressed a kiss to her temple and whispered something privately in her ear. She seemed to calm at his words.

"Your aunt did care for you." I didn't know if the words were the right thing to say, but I had to say something, so I decided on the truth. "She made so many mistakes and hurt so many people, but I do believe all of her actions came from a place of love. Perverse love, but love nonetheless. She cared for you and her grandchildren so much. I believe that."

"As do I. But thank you for saying so." Ivy sighed and pulled the blanket up over her stomach. When she looked up at me, her lips were twisted and uncomfortable. "The police said she tried to kill you?"

"Robert Wade tried to kill her," Sherborne said through clenched teeth. "Though, your aunt seemed to be the one in control of his actions. They are both equally culpable."

I laid a hand over his to steady him, and Sherborne immediately turned his hand and grabbed my fingers. Warmth spread through me until my face felt flushed.

"I'm so sorry, Alice. I had no idea she was capable of anything like that. If I'd known...poor Andrew." Ivy pressed a hand to her heart. "I did not like the man, but to be killed by his own family. And in such a manner. I can't fathom it."

The heartbreak in Ivy's eyes was plain to see. Perhaps, if I'd been able to see her face last night, I would have realized she wasn't the murderer. If eyes were the windows to the soul, Ivy's were open wide.

"And the girls," she repeated. "What will happen to them? The nanny will need to find other work, I'm sure, and they have no parents. There is no other family that can take them...not family they know, anyway. I can't begin to imagine how frightened they are. I want to go to them, but the police want me to remain in London until their investigation is through. Do you think my aunt will attempt to take me down with her?"

Questions tumbled out of her faster than anyone could possibly answer them, and John smoothed a hand down her arm. "You are innocent, Ivy. No one will be able to make you look guilty for what you haven't done."

"I will do my best to ensure that doesn't happen, as well," I assured her. "As the person nearly killed by your aunt, I think my opinion will hold some sway."

Ivy nodded, absorbing our comforting words. "But the girls..."

"They are set to inherit much of their grandmother's fortune, as are you," I said, trying to comfort her with what little information I knew. "I'm sure they will be cared for by—"

"Us."

Ivy turned to John. "What?"

"You and I," he said plainly. "We will care for the girls. As our own."

She stared at him, blinking, so he continued speaking.

"You love those children, and you would never be happy if you didn't know they were cared for and loved, so why shouldn't we do it?"

"You've never even met them, John. They don't know

you exist. How can you agree to something like this without—"

"I love you, and you love them, so I know I will grow to love them, too."

Tears brimmed in Ivy's eyes, and I felt my own vision growing misty. Suddenly, Ivy launched herself across the sofa and threw her arms around her fiancé.

Sherborne and I didn't stay much longer than that. Ivy's mood seemed markedly improved, and they had a lot to discuss about their future, so we offered our final condolences and left.

As soon as we stepped outside, Sherborne took off his jacket and laid it over my shoulders. The warmth from his body seeped into mine, and I inhaled, smelling the spicy, familiar scent of him.

"Those two seem like they will make a good pair," he said.

"They do. I hope Ivy will be happy. She deserves that."

"Don't we all." Sherborne sighed. "I think it's time we talked about our future."

I'd been walking quickly down the sidewalk, eager to get home and out of the cold, but my pace slowed until I stopped entirely. I turned to face him, and Sherborne was already looking at me.

The conversation I'd been running from for a week now had finally arrived. Sherborne had come to my house to confess his feelings, and I'd stalled as long as I could. Now, I couldn't delay anymore.

I swallowed my nerves and nodded. "Very well. Yes, we should."

Sherborne smiled even as my heart nearly raced

straight out of my chest. When he wet his lips and opened his mouth to speak, I resisted the urge to cover my ears and hum loudly to prevent myself from hearing him.

A week earlier, I would have done that exact thing. I practically did.

Now, however, I felt ready to face this. I'd stood up to my parents and the world continued spinning. And it would continue to spin whether Sherborne and I loved one another or not. I focused on that unerring truth as he began to speak.

"We have been working in close contact with one another for almost a year, and it is obvious we work well together. We balance one another out to great effect, so," he said, taking a deep breath, his chest expanding. "I think we should open a private detective agency."

I stood mute and dumb for a moment before his words fully registered and my mouth fell open. "Excuse me?"

"You've doubted yourself from the beginning of this investigation. Even Mrs. Holworthy doubted you. She hired you because she didn't believe you'd be able to unravel her crime, but you did."

"Barely," I interrupted, still unsure about where this conversation had ended up. "I nearly blamed Ivy Holworthy and got myself killed."

He waved away my argument. "You were only attacked because you figured it out and confronted Mrs. Holworthy with her crimes. Admittedly, you should have waited until I was with you to confront her, but regardless, you solved the crime, Alice. You are observant and quick and determined. Together, we could make a difference in this city."

Hadn't I just said something similar to my family at breakfast? I'd told them I enjoyed solving crimes and wanted to help people. This did seem like the path forward I'd been searching for. So, why wasn't I sure?

Probably because I'd been expecting him to confess his love for me, not offer to start a business with me. I would need a moment to readjust my expectations.

"I don't know, Sherborne."

He stepped forward and grabbed both of my hands, pulling me close to him. "I wouldn't lie to you, Alice. I hope you know me well enough by now to know that I will always tell you the truth. Even when it is inconvenient and when you don't want to hear it, I will still be honest with you. If I thought you couldn't do this, I would never suggest we go into business together. But you can. *We can.* Together."

I did believe Sherborne. He'd always told me the truth, even when it made me angry. I loved that about him. It was one of the many things I loved about him...

"You'd really want to work with me?" I asked. "Even though I am, in your own words, reckless and stubborn? Even though I tell you I'll wait for you and then run straight into danger? Even though I argue with you and—"

"Yes." He laid his hands on my shoulders and nodded his head slowly, a smile spreading across his face. "Yes to all of it, Alice. I want to work with you."

"What if we grow to hate one another?"

"That won't happen."

"How do you know?" I asked.

He narrowed his eyes and employed every drop of his charm. "I know."

Fear and uncertainty gripped my chest, but this was what I wanted. I knew it. I could feel it; a small spark of excitement growing inside of me, taking life. For some time, I'd looked at my cousin Rose's detective agency, and I'd admired it with the idea that I could never have it for myself. But why couldn't I?

"Yes."

Sherborne stepped back, expression excited, yet restrained. "Yes?"

I nodded. "Yes. I can't think of a single reason to say no, so yes. We might as well try, right?"

He grinned widely, the sharp lines of his face softening. He looked handsome. Though, he always looked handsome. "We might as well."

15

I t had been several hours since I'd made my proclamation of independence and stormed out of the house, but my family was still sitting around the table, holding the same positions they'd been in at breakfast. Except now, Charles had taken the seat next to Catherine and was bouncing Hazel on his knee.

When we walked into the room, my brother-in-law looked up and brightened noticeably. "Mr. Sherborne Sharp. It's good to see you again."

Catherine nudged Charles under the table, clearly frustrated with him for not mimicking their serious expressions, but Charles didn't seem bothered at all.

"Same to you, Mr. Cresswell. I hear you all will be in London permanently?"

"Indeed."

"Then I look forward to repaying the kindness you showed me when I came to Yorkshire," Sherborne said.

Charles agreed readily. Catherine had been telling the truth when she'd said Charles enjoyed Sherborne's company. I had a feeling the two men would be good friends in no time.

Mama cleared her throat, and Charles finally sat to attention.

"Alice. Sherborne."

"Mama," I responded in the same short tone.

"Good to see you again, Lord and Lady Ashton." Sherborne bowed.

"You left so quickly last time we didn't get to say our farewells." Papa narrowed his eyes at Sherborne, and I realized how badly I'd made Sherborne look in my family's eyes. He hadn't been in on mine and Catherine's plan to distract my family while we fled, yet it made him look disrespectful.

"That was my fault," Catherine interrupted. "I came up with that particular plot."

Charles frowned at her. "What plot?"

"Never you mind." My sister winked at me, and it felt good to know that at least she and Charles were on my side.

"You made quite a scene when you left this morning," Papa continued, barely paying Catherine any mind. "You didn't give any of us a chance to respond."

"There wasn't time. I had an appointment."

"I see that," he said, tipping his head towards Sherborne. "Mr. Sharp has been pulling you away frequently of late."

Sherborne straightened, standing even taller than he normally did.

"We are working together. I've told you that," I said.

Papa hummed, and Mama sat forward, her hands folded on the table in front of her. "You've been saying that, but I don't think any of us understood what that meant until this morning. You never told us how serious you were about your investigations, Alice."

"You never asked."

Mama bit her lip. "That is true. We've been... distracted. The last few years have been hard on all of us, and I thought...*foolishly* thought that you were handling it well. I didn't know you had questions about what happened to your brother. If I had, I would have tried to answer them."

She blinked away tears, and I could see guilt settling over her like a physical weight.

"I didn't want you to, Mama. I was fine. I am fine. I just wanted to understand how Edward had..." My voice faded, my eyes landing on my father. Out of everyone, he'd had the most difficult time dealing with Edward's crimes. They'd been close when Edward was alive. Or, at least, my father thought they had been close. Edward's crimes and betrayal had cut him deepest of all. I steeled myself and continued. "I wanted to understand how Edward had gone so far off course. And I certainly didn't want to give you anything else to worry about, so I kept my pastime to myself. I wasn't trying to be secretive. Well, maybe I was a little," I admitted with a small smile. "Mostly, I didn't want to be a burden."

"Your life is not a burden to us," Mama said. "Quite the opposite, in fact. You two girls are our entire world. We love and care for you more than you can know, and now more than ever, we want you to be honest with us."

"Do you?" I asked, turning to Papa.

He met my eyes, and for the first time in a long time, I let myself see how much he looked like Edward. They had the same coloring and face shape. If Edward had been allowed to grow old, he would have looked so much like my father.

"I'd like it if your honesty didn't happen so loudly over breakfast," he said with a huff. "But yes, I want you to be honest with me. Even if I don't like what you are saying."

Mama nodded in agreement. "You will always be a little girl to me, Alice. I will always see you as my baby. As the stubborn child who pressed her ear to her father's study door and sneaked puddings from the kitchen before dinner."

I opened my mouth to argue, but my mother held her hand up, silently asking me to let her finish.

"However, it is clear that you are a grown woman now. Regardless of how I feel about it, time has a mind of its own, and you are now an adult who is capable of making her own decisions. And I like to think we raised you well enough that those decisions will be sound ones."

"Your mother and I will support you in whatever it is you want to do," Papa added, his tone gruff, even as his words were kind. "Though, when the time comes, I will have a long, serious conversation with *whomever* it is you decide will make you happy."

His eyes landed solely on Sherborne, and I couldn't help but smile as Sherborne shifted slightly behind me, seeking shelter from my father's gaze.

My throat felt thick with tears, and I swallowed, trying to maintain my composure. All I'd wanted for as long as I could remember was for my opinion to be respected. For my family to recognize me as an adult whose contribution mattered. And now, they did.

Catherine was smiling as she looked from our parents to me, and despite my parents' disapproval this morning, it seemed as though my outburst had served its purpose. They were trying to see me as an adult, and that was all I could really ask for.

"Thank you all for your support and your confidence," I said once I'd finally ensured my voice wouldn't break. "I hope I won't do anything to lose it."

~

"You didn't tell them about our detective agency." Sherborne's jacket was still around my shoulders when we walked back outside, so he had his hands shoved into his pockets and was bouncing lightly from one foot to the other.

I raised a brow at him. "Did you want me to? I had the feeling you might rather I wait until you weren't there."

"You had the right feeling. Your father unnerves me." He tipped his head to the side in thought. "Honestly, your mother does, too."

"They are intimidating, but that's all right. As my business partner, I doubt you'll have much occasion to see them. I don't intend to entangle them in my investigations from this point on."

"As your business partner, no." Sherborne pressed his lips together and then took a step forward. Even standing on the steps while he stood on the sidewalk below, he was taller than I was. "Though, if I were more than, I might need to see them from time to time. In fact, I might even need to impress them to the point that they could begin to see me as an extended member of their family."

The heart pounding dread I'd experienced earlier when he'd mentioned the discussion of our future came back suddenly. My hands trembled, and I grabbed the lapels of Sherborne's jacket and pulled it tighter around myself.

"Alice," he continued in a low rumble. "I wanted you to agree to be my business partner before anything else because, regardless of what you say now, I think it is a good idea. We make a good team, and I think we can make a difference here in London, just as your cousin and her husband have done in San Francisco. However, to let you believe your business partner is all I want to be would be a lie. But being the great detective you are, I'm sure you've already figured that out. I've hardly made my feelings a secret."

My whole body shook now, but I didn't know why. I wasn't frightened or cold. Rather, it felt like electricity was flowing under my skin, a constant current that never seemed to run out or lose strength.

"I hope you know that your response right now will not in any way affect the plans we've already made. I wouldn't dream of turning my back on you because you do not feel as I do. Of course, I hope you will feel as I do because it would be quite awkward if you didn't." He sighed and shook his head. "I'm rambling."

"You are," I said with a laugh.

He smiled, and I could see that my good humor gave him a bit more confidence. He took a deep breath, met my eyes, and spoke plainly.

"I love you, Alice. More than I've ever loved anyone. More deeply than I ever thought possible." He shook his head. "From the moment I met you—in a rather compromising position, you might remember, since I was seconds away from stealing from your mother—you captivated me. You challenged me, intrigued me, and made me a better man."

The current under my skin began to warm, sending a flush of heat up my neck and into my face. There was also a tickle of something remarkably like butterflies in my stomach.

"I love your kind heart and the passion you have for life. I love that you never take anything at face value. You investigate and puzzle things out until you fully understand them. I love that you see things in ways I can't. And I love that every step of the way, I've had to earn your trust. You are a woman who knows what you want, and you are not afraid to turn things down in favor of something better. And even while I admire that quality, it is that quality that terrifies me right now. Because you may very well deem me unworthy of you—and rightfully, so. However, I hope—"

I leaned forward, planted my hands on Sherborne's shoulders, and pressed my lips to his.

The kiss was brief and tender, just a flutter of lips, but I felt the spark between us. The touch was enough to shift the buzzing current under my skin into something warm and liquid, something smooth and comforting that took root deep inside of me. So deeply I wasn't sure I'd ever be able to pull it free, though I didn't see why I would ever want to.

When I pulled away, Sherborne's lips were still parted in surprise, but his dark eyes had come alive. Gold swirled in his irises, reflecting the late morning light.

"You aren't unworthy," I said. "I heard you talking to

my father yesterday, and it convinced me more than anything else that you are the only man I could ever be happy with. You respect me, Sherborne. You value my opinion, and you don't want to make up my mind for me. You say that I challenge you, but you challenge me, too. The difference is that you do not block my ideas or crush my dreams. You make them better. I had nearly decided I would remain alone. I didn't see how a man would ever be able to accept me for who I am, but you have. Of course, that isn't the only reason I love you."

His eyebrows lifted. "You love me?"

I smiled and wrinkled my nose. "I'm afraid so. I love that you—"

His arms wrapped around my middle, lifting me from the step, and I let out a happy shriek as he spun me around. When he lowered me to the ground, he pressed his nose to mine.

"Don't you want to hear why I love you?"

He shook his head. "I don't care. I just care that you do. For almost a year, I've loved you, Alice. Even when I didn't know it, *I knew it.* I worried you'd never be able to forget the sneaky thief you met. Then, I worried you'd never be able to forgive me for becoming so overprotective and overbearing. For months, it has been a constant worry that I wouldn't be enough, that you wouldn't be able to return my feelings. Now, I know you feel the same way, and I can't imagine ever being happier than this."

My heart swelled, and I closed my eyes, ready to kiss him again, but a third voice broke up the happy moment.

"I wouldn't be so pleased just yet."

We sprung apart and turned to see Catherine

standing on the top of the steps, Charles lurking just behind her with a smile on his face.

"Why is that?" Sherborne asked, the huskiness gone from his voice. He was once again a proper gentleman, though I knew better.

Catherine's brow raised in a challenge. Sherborne didn't know her well—though I knew he would soon—so he couldn't see the amusement and pleasure sparkling in her eyes. He couldn't see how excited she was for her younger sister to have found someone the same way she had with Charles.

"Because," she said, lowering her chin and looking at us from behind golden lashes. "You are going to have to explain all of this to Papa."

Sherborne's face fell, and I was quick to wrap an arm around him and scowl up at my sister. "My father is nothing to worry about," I assured him. "He'll come to love you just as I do."

Catherine snorted and turned to go inside. "I'd hope that isn't true. I don't think Sherborne wants a kiss from Papa on the front steps."

I gasped, and Catherine laughed. "Honestly, you two, how are you going to start a detective agency when you can't even find a private place to—"

"Go inside, Catherine." I waved her away before she could finish her sentence.

Charles ushered Catherine inside to give us another moment alone, but he sent a wink in my direction before going indoors. He really did seem so much happier after being in the city for only a day. As annoyed as I was with both of them for interrupting this moment, I couldn't wait to spend more time with them. The four of us would be close friends, I had no doubt.

"Do you really think your father will come to like me?" Sherborne asked. "I haven't made a very good first impression."

"I'm positive he will."

He frowned. "How can you be sure?"

"Because, my love, you made a dreadful first impression on me," I reminded him. "And yet, now I love you most of all."

His cheeks colored with the memory, and he stooped and pressed a quick kiss to my cheek. "Shall we then?"

I accepted his offered arm and together, we walked up the stairs and into what was certain to be an exciting future.

Go back to where it all began. Discover the early adventures of the Beckingham family, beginning with "A Subtle Murder: A Rose Beckingham Murder Mystery, Book 1."

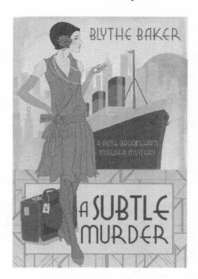

ABOUT THE AUTHOR

Blythe Baker is the lead writer behind several popular historical and paranormal mystery series. When Blythe isn't buried under clues, suspects, and motives, she's acting as chauffeur to her children and head groomer to her household of beloved pets. She enjoys walking her dog, lounging in her backyard hammock, and fiddling with graphic design. She also likes binge-watching mystery shows on TV.

To learn more about Blythe, visit her website and sign up for her newsletter at www.blythebaker.com